Lock Down Publications and Ca$h
Presents

I'mma Die Bout Mine 2
(Harder to Kill)
By: Aryanna

Lock Down Publications
P.O. Box 944
Stockbridge, GA 30281
www.lockdownpublications.com

Like our page on Facebook: Lock Down
Publications
www.facebook.com/lockdownpublications.

Stay Connected with Us!

Text LOCKDOWN to 22828 to stay up-to-date
with new releases, sneak peaks, contests and more…
Or CLICK HERE to sign up.
Like our page on Facebook:
Lock Down Publications: Facebook
Join Lock Down Publications/The New Era
Reading Group
Visit our website:
www.lockdownpublications.com
Follow us on Instagram:
Lock Down Publications: Instagram
Email Us: We want to hear from you!

Dedication:

This book is dedicated to my twin flame, Big Suge (#575628). I love u even though u a whole muthafuckin gangsta!

Acknowledgments:

First and foremost, God is great in all things that he does, so I thank him for my many blessings. I thank my family for continued support because it keeps me humbled. To my sister Big Byrd, I love u and I'm soooo proud of u. Shout out to Marcus Lee, and little Marcus who's on the way because we family for sure! Mariah Grace and Jada Boo, u know that I love u more than all the words in all the books in all the world. That'll never change. Lia, I love u more and more each day, and I miss your mom just as much. Please know that I'm always here, even when u can't see me. Aryanna, your life is your own now baby and u gotta figure out what that means because I don't get to live it for u. Imma love u regardless though, and anyone who tells u different won't say that shit to my face. On God! Kenzie, aka BIG RAIN, I love everything about your crazy ass! Lol! You're so beautiful and I pray that u realize that one day despite the bullshit Wandis has said and done to u. Shania, kenzie said hi! Thank u to my fans for their loyalty and love because I STILL do it for u the most. I fuck with u like u fuck with me. Period! I wanna thank the people that know me, who give me motivation, pep talks, and even that kick in the ass when I need it. Lol. U know who u are. LDP the game is ours! Haters, fuck U! 2024 is mine!

Chapter 1

July 2026

Life had the ability to change on a dime, which was why I was raised with the understanding that learning to adjust would be the key to my survival. That was not a lesson that you learned once and grasped. It was something that required practice that was extensive. It involved failure that was marked with blood, sweat, and tears until the ability to adjust was engrained in you like the will of breathing to live. I knew how to adjust at what life threw at me, but what I was experiencing right now was on a different wave, from a different planet. Niggas were trying to kill me, and that was nothing new. I had women issues, and that was nothing new, aside from the fact that I had multiple women pregnant at the same time. The fact that the women were related would've been enough of a reason for someone to shoot me in hopes of causing my death, but strangely enough, that wasn't one of life's problems. That fact that I'd taken a crazy nigga's chick was the side effect situation that had niggas gunning for me. I could act like I was just an innocent man being targeted for little or no reason, but then I'd be lying about the blood on my hands. I'd taken lives. Some were innocent themselves, and others just needed killing, but in both cases, I'd done what I thought was necessary and adjusted to the turns my life was taking. I didn't ask to fall in love with my high school crush. I was merely lucky in the fact of being in the right place at the wrong time. I hadn't asked to fall into a complicated situation like with that same woman's twin sister, but it was what it was, and again, I found a way to maneuver with it. It was the act of being hunted that I was scrambling to find a firm foothold with though because it was unnatural. I could admit that I wasn't the baddest muthafucka to ever walk the earth, but I was formidable when it came to getting on all bullshit. My opps knew that, so they often second guessed their decision to engage. Nobody gave a fuck right now though, which was crazy to me because I was now a man with more to lose than ever before. If my opps thought that would make me more timid or more cautious, then they must not have been thinking that shit through clearly because I was MORE dangerous now. I'd kill a man, his mama, his kids, and the family pets in order to protect and preserve my family's way of life. It was me and mine over everybody else, but I was coming to the conclusion that I was going to have to make niggas understand this from a philosophical standpoint. I was good with that though.

"Bae, where are you going?" Tynesha mumbled sleepily, reaching for my arm that had been wrapped around her.

"I'm going to get some water, sweetheart. Go back to sleep," I replied, climbing out of the king-sized bed and pulling my blue gym shorts on.

I took the time to cover her back up with the comforter and stroke her hair until her breathing deepened, and then I made my way into the kitchen.

Even though we had bottled water in the fridge, I chose to grab a glass and drink straight from the tap while looking out the balcony window. The 12th floor was a long way up for a nigga who didn't like heights, but I was still able to find some solace in the view. The clock on the microwave showed the time as 3:15 a.m., but the stars still littered the sky, creating the world's beautiful nightlight. I wasn't an overly religious person yet looking to the heavens for some type of answer seemed appropriate in this moment. I didn't know how to talk to God, so I kicked some mental words to my pops in hopes of getting guidance or advice with the direction of the next phase of the mission. The battle between those I cared about and Detective Roland Simms was over because he was dead, but beef had been inherited, and the war for me and my family's freedom raged on. I was being hunted by law enforcement, who wanted to arrest me for killing Roland, and my wife's sister, Tesha, was wanted because Roland framed her for killing the governor of Florida's son. I was still being hunted by that notorious mob known as Zoe Pound too because the cop I'd killed had been their cop. Not to mention the considerable destruction that me, my wife, Tynesha, and Tesha had caused their criminal enterprises with our little murder and robbery spree. None of what we'd done was forgiven or forgotten, and we wouldn't give a fuck if things were like they were when all of this started. Times had changed though. The moment that Tesha had revealed that she was pregnant, shit had changed for me because what my wife didn't know was that her sister's baby was mine. Their mother, Tonya, knew our secret, but her lips were sealed because my good dick had curled her toes too in our own moment of indiscretion. If that change hadn't been enough though, Tynesha discovering her own pregnancy on an accident was the biggest change in my life as of late. Fucking my wife's sister and mama was not something that I took lightly because I, for real, loved Ty with everything I had in me, and my only mission had been to be good to her and for her. Somehow, things had spiraled out of control to the point that I was about to bring two kids into a world that was unstable and unsafe. As a man and father, I knew that I needed to figure out how to balance the scales back out before I fucked up innocent lives.

"Do you ever sleep, nigga?" Shaomi asked, sneaking up behind me.

I managed not to hop out of my skin, but it was crazy that I hadn't heard her 5'1", one hundred fifteen pounds, little ass moving around in the slightest.

"I try, but sleep is an elusive whore that likes to tease a nigga," I replied, turning to face her.

The concern I felt for her pushed my eyes up to her head to see if there were signs of blood on the bandage that had her stitches covered. When her and I had almost met our end due to a well-placed car bomb meant for me, she'd suffered the more serious injury, and the guilt from that still had a hold on my heart. Shaomi being Tesha and Tynesha's first cousin made her family, but our own history as first loves was the motivation behind my need to guarantee her safety by moving her in with me and Ty. It wasn't as awkward as I'd originally feared it being but moments like accidental run-ins in the middle of the night, with her standing there in the moonlight with nothing more than a T-shirt on, were the moments I was afraid of. My life with women was complicated enough, but there had never been any closure to my relationship with Shaomi, and staring death down had a way of making things like that seem important afterwards.

"Penny for your thoughts, David?"

"Huh?" I replied, confused.

"You're staring at me, but your eyes are looking through me, and I was wondering just what you were seeing in your mind right now."

The way that she bit her bottom lip in a subconscious way was sexy as hell, and that caused me to put my glass back to my lips hurriedly. I drank real slow, just to give myself time to organize my thoughts, but the way her eyes dropped to my chest and roamed my muscles with unashamed hunger scattered them again.

"I-uh-I was just thinking about how close we both came last week to leaving this world, and that made me think about unanswered questions I still have," I said.

"What kind of questions?"

"I mean, you know, just normal shit. Like, where we went wrong," I mumbled.

"Who said we went wrong at all?"

Her response made me look at her with a squint, not fully understanding her response.

"I thought the fact that you suddenly left the state in the middle of our junior year without any explanation, or even a text to say goodbye, signaled that something was wrong," I replied, fighting to maintain my neutral tone and keep my hurt hidden.

"I know that I never apologized to you for just vanishing, but from the bottom of my heart, David, I'm sorry for leaving you. I'm even sorrier for ever hurting you because you didn't deserve that."

Her words sounded genuine, but I still felt the surprise because I definitely wasn't expecting her to offer an apology. The earnest look on her face made me think that, just maybe, she was open to actually talking about this, about us. There was only one way to find out.

"If you really mean that, then tell me why you left," I said, looking her directly in her brown eyes.

A glimpse of pain flashed across her iris like a shooting star, disappearing with a quickness that would make someone question if it was even there. She reached her hand out toward my glass, and I passed it to her. After refilling it at the sink, she returned to the spot where she'd stood in front of me and silently studied me over the rim of the glass as she drank.

"It's complicated," she said finally.

"I'm pretty smart, so I'm betting that I can keep up if you talk slow and don't use big words."

"Don't be an asshole, David. You act like this is an easy conversation to have after all this time has passed," she snapped testily.

I held up my hands in a showing of surrender before placing one hand on each of her shoulders the way that I used to when we were a couple.

"Sha Sha, it's me. It's Davie Crockett, and you know that you can tell me anything."

I thought that by invoking the memory of one of the nicknames she'd had for me that I could get her to loosen back up, but I didn't see the hint of a smile on her. The longer I stared in her eyes, the more I saw something manifest that I would've believed impossible if I weren't witnessing it. I saw her fear building.

"Talk to me, Sha Sha."

My soft request made her look around furtively, almost like she expected Ty or someone else to be eavesdropping.

I grabbed her by one hand and led her outside on the balcony, making sure to shut the door softly behind us. I wanted to say something to encourage her to speak, but my gut told me to wait because she needed to do this on her own. After a few moments, her eyes came back up to meet mine, and I saw her partially renewed courage shine through the fear.

"David, I swear to you that I didn't wanna leave, but I wasn't given a choice. First, my mom was saying that I had to go, and then, the rest of my immediate family got onboard. My grandma had the final say though, and so when she demanded that I bring my ass to Georgia, I didn't have a choice."

"But why? And why couldn't you tell me all of this then, Shaomi?"

"Because If I would've come to you to explain, I knew that you wouldn't have let me leave, and I loved you too much not to listen to you at that point in my life," she confessed.

I silently absorbed her words and their meaning, but that didn't bring as much comfort as her candid flattery probably intended.

"You were a straight A, honor roll student, who didn't get into any trouble aside from a few curfew violations as far as your family knew. So. did they find out about the shit that we were getting into in the streets?" I asked, grasping for understanding.

"No, no, it wasn't that because if that were the case, my grandma would've just killed my ass."

"Okay, so what happened? What was so fucking bad that you were forced from your home, and you couldn't tell the one man you professed undying love for?" I asked, feeling exasperated.

"David, I was pregnant by you! Now do you understand?"

Chapter 2

"Say that shit again," I demanded, trying to catch the breath that her words had knocked out of me.

My mind wanted to believe that my ears were fucked up or that the weed I'd smoked to help me sleep still had me as high as giraffe pussy. The look on her face wasn't one of a woman who'd had a slip of the tongue or one who'd said some shit just for shock value. Her eyes held an unbelievable truth that my mind wanted to deny, but my heart knew better.

"We have a four-year-old little girl named Dayjah. She lives with my grandmother right now, but I was planning to bring her to Florida once I was more stable."

"And what the fuck were you gonna tell me when I bumped into you and her out here or when word got around that you had a four-year-old? Math was my strong suit, and I'm not dumb enough to not recognize my own child when I see her," I said, hearing my voice rattle with anger.

"David, I was gonna tell you when I could actually introduce you two. Dayjah knows who her daddy is because I've showed her pictures of you and me since she was a baby, so there's no way she would've let you walk past her. I know you're mad, and you have every right to be, but please just stop for a second and think because you know how much I've always loved you. I never wanted to keep our child from you, not even for a day, but after my grandma made me leave, it just became easier to stay gone. I thought that I could forget what we were and just focus on raising our daughter because I still had a piece of our love to keep my heart beating. I knew that you'd never forgive me, so I didn't see the point in trying to explain any of this from Georgia, but Dayjah changed my mind."

"How did a four-year-old change your mind?" I asked, fighting desperately to find some sort of calm.

"Because she started asking about you constantly. She wants and needs her daddy, and that eventually pushed me to move back out here. I hadn't worked up the courage to approach you yet because I still didn't know how the fuck to tell you all of this shit, so I hid behind working to save up enough money to bring Dayjah here. Part of me believed I could just ask you for money, but I didn't wanna be THAT baby mama. I convinced myself that if you saw our daughter, you'd love her, and that would make you forgive me, but then, I started hearing crazy shit in the streets. Shit about you, Tynesha, and Tesha. I'm not blaming you for me keeping our daughter away from you. I'm just giving you a timeline to bring you up to speed on how this much time has passed."

I felt my mouth open, but nothing came out of it. Not a single sound. I took my glass back from her hands and guzzled the rest of the water in it, resisting the urge to smack her little ass over the head with it. I heard her reasoning, and I was trying to make it make sense, but all I could see was the big ass lie she'd told. My inability to see past that at this moment let me know that it was best to pause this conversation so that I didn't say or do something that I couldn't take back. Without a word, I turned around and opened the balcony door, but before I could step inside, I felt her little hand on my arm, pulling me back.

"David, please don't turn your back on me now. I know this is a tough conversation, but you did want to have it, so let's finish it."

I spun around to face her, knowing that I was giving in to the hot feeling in my chest.

"You're right. I did wanna talk, but that was before I knew you had a fucking secret this huge! You expect me to have understanding or compassion for you? I've got the same amount of both that you've had for me all of these years. You're lucky that I ain't smacked your silly ass or worst!"

"If that's what you feel that you need to do in order to be made whole on this, then by all means go ahead. You can't beat me up any worse than I have myself for the last five years, and either way, I deserve it," she admitted.

"Make me whole? The thing that makes me whole is for you to rewind time, so I don't miss a fucking day with Dayjah, and that's beyond your limited capabilities. So until you can do that, Shaomi, I would suggest that you just stay the fuck away from me and let me think."

"David, what's going on?" Ty asked from behind me.

The instant fear that appeared on Shaomi's face coincided with my stomach dropping like an elevator from the thirtieth floor, but I knew that I couldn't give in to the feeling of rising panic. I gave Shaomi a look intended to tell her to keep her muthafuckin mouth shut because there was no way I was about to tell Ty what we were just discussing.

"Baby, what are you doing up?" I asked, changing my whole demeanor as I spun back around.

"I heard your voice in my sleep, and I wanted to make sure that you were okay. What the hell are you and Shaomi out here arguing about in the middle of the night?"

"Nothing important. Come on," I said, lying while leading her back to the bedroom.

I put the empty glass on the nightstand before helping her back in between the warmth of the comforter and the sheets.

"David, why are you treating me like I'm fragile just because I'm pregnant now?"

"I'm not, bae. I'm just being an attentive husband," I replied, forcing a smile on my face as I slid into bed next to her.

I pulled her close to me and held her while trying to slow down the Ferrari racing through my mind with a million dollars' worth of questions.

"David?"

"Yeah, babe?"

"You love me, right? I mean, you're still in love with me and not regretting your decisions?" she asked softly.

"Of course I'm still in love with you, baby, and I don't regret a damn thing about us. I'm fucked up about you, and that'll never change, so where are these questions coming from?"

"It's just... I know that a lot happened in a short amount of time, and that doesn't give you time to process all of your emotions. I know what you and Shaomi were to each other in high school because I secretly envied it, so I can only imagine the emotional turmoil that her being under the same roof has caused you," she replied.

Immediately, my heart stopped beating in my chest because fear had seized it. It might have been naïve of me to think that Ty didn't know about her cousin's baby, which would've led her to the logical conclusion about who Dayjah's father was. The only thing that I didn't understand was why Ty hadn't told me before now because she didn't seem like the type to be okay with keeping a kid away from someone who'd be a good father.

"What Shaomi and I were is in the past, baby, and I told you that before we agreed on this living arrangement of having her up here with us instead of downstairs with your mom and Tesha. I won't lie. There were unanswered questions about what happened and why she just left five years ago, and that's the conversation that you walked up on. There's nothing that could jeopardize us or my love for you though. Absolutely nothing," I said, hoping to reassure her while temperature checking her simultaneously.

"I understand, babe, and I get you having unanswered questions because, honestly, we all did. It was never explained why she was called home to Georgia, only that her grandmother needed her close. We just figured that her

16

grandmother must be sick, and she was gonna take care of her until she passed away, but then, she popped back up last year. And she was... different. I don't know how to explain it except to say that Shaomi came back a completely different woman than the girl who left. You remember that she used to party with us, and me, her, and Tesha were inseparable, but me and Tesha ain't really seen her since she's been back. If she's not working, then she's going back-and-forth to Georgia on the regular. That's part of the reason I was surprised she agreed to get involved with everything we had going on with Roland and them Zoe Pound niggas. It's obvious that she did it for you though and that she stayed because of you. I'm just wondering if you can see it or if you're ignoring it?"

"Neither. I think she's here for the money I promised her and because you're her family, not because we had a relationship when we were kids," I replied in what I hoped was a convincing tone of voice.

Ty didn't argue against my reasoning and explanation, but her silence made it obvious that she still had more to say on the subject. I wasn't about to force it out of her. Instead, I wanted to banish any thoughts she still had about me not loving her and wanting her. When I pulled her on top of me, she didn't resist, and the moment that our lips touched, I felt the familiar electricity bond our souls together. My hands quickly pulled the T-shirt that she was wearing up and over her head so that I could feel the heat of her soft skin pressed against my own. She wasted no time snaking her hand inside my shorts and pulling my rapidly hardening dick out so that she could straddle me. Seconds later, I felt the most beautiful sensations of warmth and wetness surround me as I was submerged inside her tight pussy walls. Every feeling was as foreign as it was familiar, but I was only focused on mutual satisfaction. I kept my hands on her juicy ass cheeks even though the slow rhythm of rise and fall was of her own design because I was good with giving her control. I'd learned early on that her 5′6″, one hundred forty-five pounds could take the punishment I was known to deliver but taking it nice and slow sometimes was the best approach. Our kisses of passion were synchronized with her sensually riding me, which only made the temperature we created hotter and more dangerous. I let my fingers walk up her body ever so slowly and deliberately, in a way that alternated between feather light touches and a firmness that would leave my prints on her beautiful flesh. I loved how something so simple could make her heart pound. By the time my hands were fixed on her backbone, pulling her closer to me, she willingly molded herself to my body like we'd always been in the same skin. My mouth caught her every moan like hers did my every sigh, but still our love making wasn't quiet. Her pussy grip created enough pressure that the suction it created could be heard every time she slid more than halfway off my dick.

At the same time, my hips rising to meet hers created the sounds of someone diving into the depth of a whirlpool as her pussy juices splashed wildly with my every thrust. We existed within this ocean of our primal nature until neither of us could fight the inevitable. Her sudden movement of sitting up straight on the dick had me knocking on her walls from a different angle, and when she swiveled her hips like a washer on spin cycle, I bout lost my damn mind.

"Fuck me, baby," she whispered seductively, putting both of her hands on my chest. She continued to swivel like a joystick as I rammed dick up inside of her like I was trying to make her head touch the ceiling. Within minutes, we were both harmonizing climaxes like our shadows dancing on the wall were paying spectators. My dick was still throbbing as she collapsed on my chest, but her grip didn't loosen in the slightest until she'd snatched every drop of my life's force. Our silence was one of happiness and love, but even in this moment, I could feel my hidden truth still pulling at my conscience. I desperately wanted to talk to Ty about it because she was my best friend, and I needed that right now, but it would've been selfish of me to unload this secret with so little supporting information. The bottom line was that I needed to know the whole truth before I could bring it to the light of day, and there was only one way to get that. Slowly, a plan began to take shape in my mind, and by the time Ty started her beautiful light snoring, I knew what to do. I was careful with my movements because moving her from my chest to the bed could cause her to wake up if I did it too fast. Once I had her lying beside me, I slowly crept out of bed, and then, I made a mad dash into our walk-in closet. Ten minutes later, I emerged, fully dressed in a navy-blue track suit, carrying my Sig Sauer P290 .223 Carbine with the one hundred round drum on it, and I headed to the room where Shaomi slept. To my surprise, she wasn't sleep at all, and our eyes locked as soon as I turned the corner into the room.

"Fucked your girl to sleep and now you come to kill me?" she asked, smiling mischievously.

"Shut up, get dressed, and come on."

"Where are we going?" she asked, not moving at all.

"To Georgia. We're going to see our daughter."

Chapter 3

(Tynesha)

I knew that I wasn't dreaming because I could feel the hunger pains making themselves known in my stomach's rumbles, but I also felt the smile on my face. Never in my twenty-one years could I ever remember literally waking up with a smile on my face and I didn't even have to question why I had one now because instinctively I knew the answer. Love. I was in a love so rare with my own husband that half the time its intensity terrified me, and the other half of the time I spent trying to catch my breath because I was so fucking giddy! There was nothing anyone could've told me six months ago that would've made me believe a love like this existed or that it would be mine for the taking. At that point in my life, things had been so emotionally bad with my ex, Roland, that I really didn't believe in the idea of love, let alone the institution of it that led to marriage and children. I'd honestly just been trying to survive the foolish decision I'd made but eventually not even that was enough, and I found myself at a point so low that death was all I wanted to embrace. David had saved my life in more ways than one that day at the gas station, and the best part was that he did it just because it was who he was. Even before I knew him as intimately as I did now, I knew that he wasn't perfect, but he was still a damn good man. That was a reason for any lucky woman to go to sleep and wake up with a smile on their face, and I was blessed to now forever be that woman.

I opened my eyes, hoping to catch a glimpse of my man still sleeping, because he was so damn cute in those moments, but immediately, I was greeted by the disappointing sight of his spot being empty. Naturally, my nose searched the air, but I didn't smell food or weed, and that was enough to pull me from beneath the warmth of the comforter. I had a moment's pause when I felt something sticky in between my thighs, and my heart beat faster in fear. A quick check revealed still drying cum and not blood, and the reason made me chuckle with relief as I headed for the shower. I would find David after that. I spent countless minutes washing my body, imaging his strong hands tracing the same route, and by the time my shower was over, I was completely soaking wet from the inside out. As hungry as I was, my craving had switched that fast, and I needed to be fed another serving of good dick with a side of that head he'd become an expert at giving. I dried off quickly and threw on another one of his big t-shirts without panties or a bra so that he didn't have to work hard to get what he wanted.

"Oh, Daaavvviiiddd!" I sang out sensually, damn near skipping into the living room.

I'd expected him to be sitting in front of the eighty-inch, plasma screen T.V. on the wall, playing his PlayStation 7 alone or with Shaomi, but the living room was as empty as our bed had been. A search of the dining room, balcony, and kitchen turned up the same results, which forced my eyes into the one direction that I didn't want to look in. My mama had taught me long ago that if you asked a question then you had to be prepared to do something with the answer. Whether that was accepting the answer or acting a goddamn fool, you still had to do something because you couldn't ignore what you asked to know once you knew it.

"David?" I called out, loud enough to be heard anywhere in the apartment.

I hoped he would answer. I just didn't want that answer to come from behind the closed door of Shaomi's room, which my eyes were currently fixed on. I trusted David, even knowing his past with my cousin, but the argument I'd walked up on between them was heated, and my gut had told me that there was more to the story than what he'd said.

Could both of them really be crazy enough and disrespectful enough to actually be fucking in the next room while I was asleep? I didn't know, but if I was going to ask the question, then I had to be ready to deal with the answer. That thought sent me back into the bedroom that David and I shared and into the closet's safe. I punched in the code from memory, grabbed the first gun my hand touched, and then I shut the door back. I checked the clip and pulled the slide on the Taurus .45 as I was walking back to Shaomi's room, pausing briefly outside of her closed door. I hesitated for half a second and no more.

"Fuck that," I said, opening the door wide with the pistol out in front of me.

My heart beat slowed down a little when I didn't immediately spot them in a compromising position on the bed, but I switched my focus to the bathroom and approached it the same way. Finding it empty as well brought me back to the bed, which had obviously been slept in, and I felt like it was taunting me somehow. The crazy bitch in me wanted to smell the sheets because I knew my nigga's scent whether he was sweating or not, but I resisted the urge. On my way out of the room, I spotted the t-shirt that Shaomi had been wearing the last time I saw her, and that sent me back to my room. A search revealed that David had gotten dressed too, and the Sif Sauer P290 .223 Carbine was gone as well. All of this added up to them leaving the apartment, and more likely the building, so my next move was to check all logical places for a note. It took less than ten minutes for a bitch to go from curious to pissed because I couldn't find a note anywhere, and that led to me pulling on some sweats and my black Air Maxes. I made sure to tuck the pistol on me before leaving the apartment and taking the elevator down to David's other apartment on the ground floor. Since he'd made my DNA and fingerprints part of his security protocol, I didn't need to knock on the door. I simply put my thumb on the scanner by the lock and turned the knob. When the smell of bacon hit my nose, my stomach wasted no time reminding me that I was running on borrowed time before lack of nourishment became an intolerable issue.

"Ma?" I called out.

"In the kitchen," Tesha replied.

I followed the sound of my twin's voice, and I found her sitting at the kitchen counter next to our mother, who was at the stove showing out.

"Hey, baby, you hungry?" my mom asked.

"You know that bitch hungry, Ma. Look at her fat ass nostrils flaring like she's tasting the air and shit," Tesha said, cackling with laughter.

"Are David and Shaomi down here?" I asked, ignoring the small talk.

Some sort of look flew in between my mother and sister, causing me to immediately grab the pistol and sit it in front of me as I took a seat at the kitchen table.

"Since when did you start walking around with guns on you?" Tesha asked, no longer laughing.

"Since my nigga and his ex both disappeared without an explanation. So, I'mma ask you both again. Are they here?"

"No, they ain't here, baby," my mom replied, putting a plate of food in front of me.

The crisp bacon, fluffy scrambled eggs, and cinnamon roll distracted me instantly, and I picked up the fork before it could get comfortable on the table beside the plate. I was so consumed by the punishment that I was putting on the food that I didn't even realize I was being watched until I heard laughter.

I looked up to find my mother and sister shaking their heads as they looked at me eating, and they kept right on laughing.

"What?" I asked self-consciously around a mouthful of eggs.

"Breathe, bitch!" Tesha said, laughing harder.

"That's definitely a boy you're carrying because your ass is picking up weight as fast as you are that damn fork you're using like a snow shovel," my mom said.

"Forget you both," I replied, focusing back on my food.

I kept right on fucking shit up like I was racing to get back in line at the buffet before the Chinese spareribs ran out. By the time my mom had her plate fixed and the stove turned off, I had only crumbs left, and I was feeling fat and happy. The happy part vanished once my eyes landed on the pistol beside my plate, and I remembered the original mission.

"I don't understand why the hell David would leave the building without telling me, especially knowing that he's a fugitive with a bounty on his head," I said aloud, shaking my head in confusion.

Out of the corner of my eye, I saw Tesha give our mom that look again, and I jumped on it swiftly.

"What do the two of you know that I don't? It's no use denying it because ain't neither one of you built to play poker so just spit the shit out," I demanded impatiently.

"You're not gonna like it," Tesha warned.

"And?" I asked, fighting my anxiety.

"There was some type of emergency in Georgia that required Shaomi to go back asap... so David took her," my mom said.

"He... What?" I asked slowly, struggling to wrap my mind around what I'd heard.

"With her fresh off that head wound and him feeling guilty because that car bomb was meant for him, are you really surprised that David would make sure that she got to Georgia safely?" Tesha asked in an attempt to sound rational.

"I mean, yeah, but... what happens if..."

I couldn't even finish speaking the question aloud because in my heart, I knew that I didn't want that answer. I didn't want a damn thing in the world except for my husband to walk through that fucking door right now.

"He'll be okay, baby. If I've learned one thing in the time that I've known David, it's that he can take care of himself," my mom said with a sincere smile.

My mind went back to the night that he'd had to save her life because shooters had descended on our family home with death's intentions. He'd managed to keep both of them alive and get them out of harm's way that night, but that knowledge only brought minimal comfort. All it took was one bullet, and my world would come to a screeching halt because I wasn't prepared to live without him. I didn't know how.

"What the fuck happened in Georgia to make Shaomi risk the trip? I mean, she knows how crazy shit is for all of us right now, so did somebody die?" I asked.

"I honestly don't know. All that they said was that Shaomi got the call, and it was serious enough to have them on the road within minutes," Tesha replied.

"Fuck all this vague shit. I wanna know what this silly ass bitch just dragged my man into. Ma, call your sister because I'm telling you now that cousin or not, I'mma beat that bitch if it ain't life or death," I vowed passionately.

"Shit, I'm with you, sis," Tesha said with seriousness and an edge in her tone.

Surprisingly, our mom didn't say a word. She just pulled her phone out of her shorts pocket and began to dial.

"Put it on speaker," I demanded.

"Little girl, chill," she replied, putting the phone to her ear and waiting.

It was in my heart to argue, but I took the win instead for her making the call in the first place, and I waited with my mouth shut.

"What's up, Tierra? It's Tonya... yeah, your sister, Tonya, bitch. Who else? Is everything okay down there because Shaomi took off like a bat out of hell to get back to Georgia, and all she told us was that it was an emergency... Okay, I'll wait," my mom said, holding her index finger up to head off any questions I was about to send her way.

The seconds ticked by loudly and slowly, so much so that after a few minutes of silence, I noticed my mom's own impatience in her fingers tapping rhythmically on the counter.

"Yeah, I'm here, Tee... Okay, well, who is that because I don't know anyone in the family by that name? Oh... Oh, shit," my mom said, pulling the phone away from her ear.

She closed her eyes for the briefest of moments, and I prepared myself to hear the bad news about a distant relative passing.

"What is it, Mom?" Tesha asked.

Our mom looked at her and just shook her head, but it wasn't until she turned her green-eyed stare on me that I felt butterflies kick my stomach.

"Mom... what is it?" I asked, echoing my sister.

"Sh-Shaomi had to get back home to see Dayjah."

"Who's Dayjah?" Tesha asked before I could.

My mom opened her mouth to speak, but it was like the words got stuck or something, causing her to spin wildly and vomit straight in the sink.

"Oh, shit, Mom, are you okay?" I asked, hopping up.

I reached her side just in time because she collapsed into me, and I had to plant my feet to avoid us both attacking the floor.

"Are you okay?" I asked, concerned.

"Yeah, I'm just-I'm just..."

"You're pregnant," Tesha said.

I damn near burst into laughter at what my sister said until I realized that our mom hadn't corrected her.

"Mom, y-you're pregnant? How? Who?" I stammered, completely mind blown.

26

"Yeah, Mom, who's your baby daddy?" Tesha asked, smiling mischievously.

Chapter 4

(David)

The drive had been full of tense and strained silences for the first few hours, but I eventually got Shaomi to loosen up by asking her some questions about Dayjah. Even as I absorbed the information, it was still hard for me to process that I had a four-year-old little person walking the earth. When Shaomi finally showed me a picture of her, the truth became undeniable because I was looking into eyes the same color light brown and shape of my own. She had her mom's nose and ears, but the longer I looked at the picture, the more features of my face I saw on our little girl. Once we'd hit the Georgia state line, I'd switched seats with Shaomi and let her drive, in part because she had a license from this state and because she knew where we were going. Logically, I should've been dead tired and sleeping while she drove, but I was too anxious for that for real.

"How much farther?" I asked once I saw the welcome sign to Macon, Georgia.

"Not far, about ten more minutes. If you keep asking me though, I'mma take the long way home."

When I looked over to see if she was serious, I caught the smirk pulling at the corner of her mouth. A huge part of me was still mad at her, but the logical side continued to argue against that for the sake of our child. The last thing that I wanted was for our baby to pick up on our tension and see any type of unhealthy interactions in our relationship. A lesson that I'd learned the hard way growing up was that how your parents interacted affected a child's innocence, especially if they couldn't hide their bias. I didn't have to physically see my parents fight in order to know that my mother had no love or respect for my stepfather, and that influenced my feelings greatly. Until I learned the truth. I wanted to give our daughter a clean slate to paint her own vision of her parents, and for me, that started with my actions.

"Hey, uh, I just wanted to thank you before things got crazy," I said.

"Thank me for what?"

"For agreeing to make the trip immediately and for... for raising Dayjah on your own when it probably would've been easier to have an abortion," I replied, glancing over at her.

"You don't gotta thank me for either thing. It's beyond time for you two to meet, and you should already know that I love you too much to ever kill a child we created."

I started to correct her speech because she'd used the word love in the present context instead of the past, but she spun two quick left turns, and we came to a stop. I could feel my heartbeat quicken, and the air suddenly tasted different than it had seconds prior.

"Do-Do you want me to wait here?" I asked.

When Shaomi looked over at me, I could see surprise contorting all of her facial features, and then, she chuckled softly.

"Nigga, I watched you get us out of the mouth of death not too long ago without any fear, but now you're damn near trembling over a little girl? Awww... get your soft ass out of the car," she demanded, laughing at me as she got out.

I was able to laugh at myself because there was a lot of truth to what she said, and that helped to lessen my anxiety somewhat as I climbed out of the car. The sun was high in the sky on this beautiful day, but the temperature was just right when compared to Florida's humidity. The house we'd pulled up to was big with three levels, and it sat on a nice plot of land that was at least an acre away from any neighbor on either side. Anything below Tennessee was considered southern, but there was a difference between Florida southern and Georgia southern. I could feel it in the air. Shaomi stood in front of the car, looking around for a few moments, and then, she signaled for me to follow her lead inside. My footsteps felt heavier than usual, like my Kobes had cement laces or heels full of lead, but I forced them to keep moving. It was midafternoon, but I didn't see any movement when my eyes drifted through the ground floor window. Shaomi didn't bother knocking. She just opened the door, and we stepped inside the foyer where cool air greeted us.

"Ma?" Shaomi called out.

I didn't hear a response, but she kept us moving forward, like someone was talking to her in spirit or something, until we came to a living room at the back of the house.

"Mommy!" I heard someone squeal.

Shaomi stopped in her tracks and kneeled down to catch then little girl racing in her direction, but the moment those light brown eyes landed on me, she came to a screeching halt. I would've recognized Dayjah anywhere in the world and based on the light of recognition that suddenly glowed in her eyes, I knew that Shaomi had told me the truth about our daughter knowing me. I stood frozen, not knowing what the fuck to do but not wanting to do anything that would affect Dayjah in a bad way. She looked me up and down twice, and then, her eyes swung back to her mom.

"Is-Is that my daddy?" she asked softly.

Even with her low tone, I could still hear the hope in her question, and it partially broke my heart because it told me just how much she wanted me. The love that suddenly swelled inside my chest was foreign but so consuming that I found myself on my knees beside Shaomi. Dayjah took a tentative step in my direction, as if she was unsure of my reaction to her invasion of my bubble. Instinctively, I threw my arms open wide, and that was all the invitation she needed.

"Daddy!" she screamed, flinging herself into my arms hard enough to knock me backwards and make me laugh.

We gave each other kisses until it felt like my face was covered in saliva, but I knew that there were plenty of tears mixed into the moisture. When I looked up, Shaomi was standing over us with her hand pressed to her mouth, sobbing silently despite the happiness that was burning bright in her eyes. I reached my hand out to her, and when she took it, I pulled her down on top of Dayjah and me, bringing us together as a family for the first time.

"Mommy, you found Daddy!" Dayjah yelled over and over, hugging me before using her fingers to trace the lines of my face.

"I promised you that I would, baby, and Mommy keeps her promises. Right?"

"Right!" Dayjah yelled excitedly.

"Dayjah, why are you making all that noise?" a woman asked, entering the room out of my line of sight.

Shaomi rolled off of us, and I sat up quickly, spotting her grandmother standing a few feet away. It had been years since I'd seen her, but I remembered that her relationship with Shaomi was more of a mother-daughter bond. This was the lady who'd raised her, taught her, and ultimately protected her by giving her some of life's harshest lessons in a crash course. It was no wonder that she called her grandmother *Mama* and referred to her mom by first name most of the time.

"D-David, is that you?"

"Yes, Ms. Web, it's me."

Her eyes went to Shaomi before coming back to me and Dayjah, who was clinging to me with clear intentions of not letting go anytime soon.

"Well, it's about time," Ms. Web said, smiling.

"Mama, don't start please," Shaomi said, standing up.

I figured out how to awkwardly get to my feet without letting Dayjah go, and I took a step in front of Shaomi so that I was standing between her and her grandmother.

"The past is the past, and all that matters is all of us moving forward with the same desire to see Dayjah happy, healthy, and loved. I appreciate all the help that you gave Shaomi and Dayjah. As soon as we get back to Florida, I'll send enough money to cover the expenses for the last five years," I vowed.

"You're very welcome, but that's my great-granddaughter so nothing that I did was about anything other than my love for her and Shaomi. You don't gotta pay nobody back except for that little girl in your arms because that's who you both owe for life. Just be there for her, okay?"

"Yes, ma'am," I replied readily.

"Always have been and I always will be," Shaomi said, rubbing Dayjah's back gently.

When I looked at Shaomi, I saw all the love that I knew we both felt for our daughter, but that didn't hide the fear. I understood now why she'd agreed to team up with us for the money because providing for Dayjah's future was a priority for me now too. Keeping us all alive was priority number one though and that wasn't as easy as it would've been a few weeks ago.

"Daddy, I made a lot of stuff for you," Dayjah said, pointing toward a hallway that I assumed led to her bedroom.

"Show me," I said, putting her down on her feet.

She wasted no time taking off at a full sprint in the direction she'd pointed. I waited until she was out of earshot before I turned to address Shaomi and her grandmother.

"We're gonna take her back to Florida. I can't protect her from here, and I refuse to leave my daughter vulnerable."

"Protect her from who? What type of trouble are you two in this time?" Ms. Web asked, looking back-and-forth between me and Shaomi.

"It's a long story, Ma, but David is right. We're taking her with us."

"And then what, Shaomi? You wanna take my great-granddaughter straight into the lion's den where danger is? How the fuck does that make sense?! This was the exact reason we made you leave Florida in the first place, and you know that."

"It makes sense because the apartment building we live in is the safest place in the world right now. No one can get in, not even the Feds, without our permission. I know why you made me leave, but things are different now, and we can handle it," Shaomi replied.

"That's all fine and dandy for now, but what happens when or if whoever you have problems with decides to bring the whole building down, killing you that way? That building is only as safe as the minds of the lunatics you're mixed up with! Don't you realize that?"

Her questions had us looking at each other in bewilderment because neither of us had considered someone trying to knock the fucking building down. Right now, no one knew we were there, but the moment that changed then what Shaomi's grandmother suggested became a real issue that needed considering.

"Daddy?" Dayjah called.

"Here I come, sweetie."

"Go ahead. We've got time to figure out our next move before we make it. Right now, our daughter needs you, and you need her," Shaomi said, squeezing my hand gently.

I nodded my head before I dropped a quick kiss on her forehead and followed the sound of Dayjah's voice. When I came around the corner, I immediately saw my little girl sitting on the carpet covered bedroom floor surrounded by drawings, handmade cards, and a few stuffed animals scattered in the mix.

"What's this?" I asked, sitting down beside her.

"I made drawings for you, and I kept them like Mommy said until you came home from school. You were at school a long-time, Daddy, so please don't go back," she said, looking at me with an expression of hope entwined with fear blanketing her beauty and innocence.

I pulled her onto my lap and just held her, inhaling the strawberries and bubble gum scent on her skin and storing it in my mind. I never knew that a love could exist without reason or explanation. In truth, I didn't know my daughter, but I loved her with my whole heart, and I'd stop a bullet for her. My love for her was as pure as it was unconditional, and the feelings surrounding that love were only made stronger with every second we spent together. I didn't know how much time we spent on her bedroom floor before I felt the presence of someone else, but I looked up to find Shaomi standing in the doorway watching us.

"Your lunch is ready, Dayjah. Go to the kitchen and see your grandma," Shaomi said.

Instantly, Dayjah froze and looked up at me, her eyes alight with a fear that I understood right away.

"I'll still be here when you're done, sweetheart," I said, giving her a hug and a kiss.

My reassurance put that huge smile back on her face before she took of running at top speed from the room.

"She has your energy, I swear," Shaomi said, shaking her head and smiling ruefully.

"Shit, that ain't all me because your little ass stayed on the move when we were younger. She's amazing though."

"Yeah, she is... Listen, David, I'm sorry for..."

"It's okay, Sha Sha, and you don't have to apologize anymore because I meant it when I told your grandmother that I'm all about moving forward. I would rather focus on what we gotta do to keep her safe," I said.

"I agree, and I just had a LONG conversation with my grandmother about that, convincing her that we knew how to be good parents now. There's something else that you should know though. Ty had her mom call my mom, and my mom told her why we'd made the sudden trip to Georgia."

I felt my smile vanish as the magnitude of her words took hold and burrowed into my brain.

"What exactly did your mom say?" I asked slowly.

"Enough for Tonya to know that I came to Georgia to see my daughter and you know like I do what the next logical question will be."

"Who's your baby's daddy," I said, bowing my head.

Chapter 5

(Tynesha)

"You still look like you might pass the fuck out, Ma, so why don't you let me run you upstairs to the doctor real quick?" I suggested.

"Last time I'm gonna say it to the both of you. I'm fine, and I don't need no damn doctor," she replied, sliding onto a bar stool at the kitchen counter.

The look that I gave Tesha called cap on the 'I'm fine' shit that our mother was feeding us, but if she wanted to play then I was up for a round of twenty-one questions.

"So, who knocked your old ass up?" I asked.

"Why the fuck do you two keep insisting that I'm pregnant? You do know that people vomit for other reasons, right?" she asked sarcastically.

"You're absolutely right, Mom. People blow chunks for all sorts of reasons not related to pregnancy... BUT you've managed to do it only in the morning for the past few mornings," Tesha pointed out.

"I don't know what you're talking about, child," she replied with a straight face.

"Oh, really, Mother? So, you must think that just because you turn the shower on that the sounds of water somehow smother the sounds of gagging?" Tesha asked, laughing at the look of guilt on our mom's face.

"You're hearing shit, Tesha, and I suggest you let it go before I grill your ass about who your baby's daddy is," she replied.

I chuckled at the two of them going back-and-forth until I realized that I didn't know who Tesha's baby daddy was. In all the confusion and chaos, my focus had been everywhere but on Tesha and her situation, but now, it was time to think and be nosy.

"You bring up a good point, Ma, because the bitch ain't even told me which nigga with good dick she let dump cum in her to get her pregnant," I said, looking pointedly at my twin.

She blushed a shade of hot pink before her eyes swung toward our mom, and I knew to keep on pressing.

"Come on, twin, who..."

"Actually, you got bigger issues to think about and work through right now," Mom said seriously.

"What are you talking about?" I asked as my mind shifted from playful to wary.

"Shaomi's mom said that they went to Georgia to check on Dayjah, and I was in the middle of telling you and Tesha that."

"I heard that part, but I still don't remember any Dayjah in our family," Tesha replied.

"Me either," I echoed.

"I didn't know who she was either until I asked your auntie. Dayjah is Shaomi's daughter."

I'd been watching my mother's lips move, so I knew that she'd spoken in a regular tone, but for some reason, the word daughter came out hella loud. The look on Tesha's face told me that she felt the same way I did.

"When the fuck did Shaomi have a kid?" Tesha asked.

"Apparently it's been a while ago because her daughter is four years old," Mom replied, looking directly at me.

Without me even issuing a request, my mind began to work the math equation to this new mystery, and my heart froze with the answer.

"It was five years ago that she disappeared to Georgia without any explanation," I said.

"Now we know why," Tesha commented, shaking her head with an expression of disbelief on her face.

"Did David ever mention this to you?" Mom asked, looking at me.

"Not directly, no, but now, it puts their argument at three o'clock in the damn morning into perspective. He'd said that they'd been talking about the past, but he didn't give me any details. He just..."

My voice trailed off as thoughts of my last moments spent with David flashed through my mind like a porn reel.

"He must've dicked you down because that faraway look in your eyes only happens with a really good distraction technique," Tesha said.

I didn't waste time denying the truth in her statement because it would've exposed how used I felt in this moment. I kept my focus on the fact that my husband had a baby with my cousin.

"Ma, you didn't know?" I asked, just to be sure.

"Hell nah, or I would've spoke on it years ago! We don't hide no damn kids in this family because I damn sure took it on the chin when it came to my being pregnant with you two."

"Why do you think Shaomi hid her daughter then?" Tesha asked.

"I don't know, but I'm damn sure gonna ask her when she gets back," I vowed.

"You all are family, which means that you ain't fighting behind no nigga. David and Shaomi had a baby together, and that baby is related to all of us, so we not bout to start no shit. Understand?" Mom asked, looking at Tesha first and then me.

"I'm cool, Ma, but your girl looks pissed," Tesha said, nodding in my direction.

"I'm good, but that nigga gonna catch this fade for lying to me because he knows better," I replied.

"Men lie, women lie, so don't expect different," Mom said.

There was wisdom in her words, but I couldn't ignore how his lies made me feel.

"A marriage is built in transparency though, Ma, and we had that conversation, so like I said, that nigga know better," I stated stubbornly.

"If he was your husband, then you could probably take that approach, but he's your baby daddy, sis, which means he thinks he can get away with half-truths," Tesha said.

I opened my mouth to correct her, and then, I realized that I'd almost slipped up and let the cat out of the bag. No one on my side of the family knew that David and I had gotten married in L.A. or that his family was African royalty. We'd kept it between us, but now, I was questioning why since it seemed like everybody had secrets that only proved damaging when kept in the dark.

"I taught you girls a long time ago that even God keeps secrets, so you should always expect men and women to lie. That doesn't change just because you're in love with a nigga or because the dick is good," Mom stated.

"Marriage wouldn't change it either, and I doubt that David is the marrying kind," Tesha said, smirking.

Without saying anything, I held up my hand so that they could see the rings on my left hand.

"Yeah, we noticed you sporting those when you two came back from your west coast trip, but even if he asked, that don't mean he's ready right now," Tesha persisted.

"These rings ain't for show. We really got married when we were in Cali."

"That's bullshit," Tesha said, laughing and shaking her head.

"Why would you not tell us that or invite us?" Mom asked.

"It was something that happened in the heat of the moment, Ma. David didn't even plan it. It was his aunt and uncle that made the shit happen," I replied honestly.

"Like some kind of arranged marriage?" Mom asked.

"Yes and no. I wasn't forced to marry him. It was my choice. I was given the option of doing it right then and there as a demonstration of the love and loyalty I'd proclaimed when it came to David. So, we did it."

"You're serious? Tynesha, you, for real, married that nigga?" Tesha asked.

Her disbelief merged with her anger to create a weird expression on her face.

"I swear to you on the soul of my unborn baby that David and I are legally married in real life."

"Un-fucking-believable!" Tesha said, hopping up and storming out of the room.

"Tesha, wait..."

"Let her go," Mom said softly.

"I don't get why she's that mad though, Ma. I get that I didn't tell her, but shit, I didn't tell anyone."

"That don't seem crazy to you, that you didn't tell us? Come on, Tynesha, you've never been secretive with your twin or me for the most part. I know that there's certain things that you can't or won't tell your mom, and that's okay, which is why I've never pushed to know everything going on in either of your lives. Your relationship with her is a different story. You two are twins and have moved like one since I put you side by side in the crib together. That bond has withstood every test or obstacle that either of you has been up against because you two learned early on that nobody could love you more than each other. Ever since you and David started fucking around though, you been moving way different, and I'm sure that's hurting Tesha."

"Ma, that's crazy, and you know it. Can't no nigga, no matter how good the dick is, make me forget the bond I have with my twin or with you, and y'all know that shit. You already know that things change when any of us are in a

40

serious relationship but not to the point that my loyalty to family should be in question because I would never question either of you like that. On top of that, David ain't just some random nigga that I'm fucking. That man is my person, and I felt that connection long before we exchanged vows. I would expect you and Tesha to be happy for me because you understand that a love like this is more than rare. This love is right, Ma. So, I get that I may be moving a little different now that I'm with him, but that don't mean that I've switched up on you or her. Damn, you make it sound like my energy is real oppy or something," I said, screwing up my face in frustration.

"I'm not taking it that far, sweetheart. I'm just saying that your sister is entitled to feel like you've changed because you have. That truth is undeniable."

I knew that my mom and I could go back-and-forth all day on this topic, but the problem was between me and Tesha, so I politely excused myself and went to find her. I smelled the weed as soon as I hit the hallway, and it pulled me in the direction of her bedroom. I could hear her voice coming through the door, but I knew that no one could be in there with her, so I opened the door. She was sitting on the bed with her phone in one hand and a blunt in the other, which was typical. The way she jumped up after disconnecting her call was weird though.

"I didn't mean to interrupt your phone call, but we need to talk real quick. What the hell is going on with you?"

"I'm good, just hormonal as fuck. Don't pay me no mind," she replied.

"I know you better than that so kick that real shit to me, sis, and tell me what the problem is."

"I told you that I'm good, and we're good. I was just surprised to hear that you actually married David. That shit is wild but congrats for real," she said, hitting the blunt.

"Why is it wild? Ma said you feel like I've changed since I got with him, but I wanna hear that come out of your mouth. How have I changed?"

"Ty, just let it go and enjoy life with the man you love. Don't worry about what Ma was saying because everyone changes. I love you no matter what," she said, passing me the blunt.

I wanted to smack the blunt out of her hand, but I couldn't disrespect the weed, so I took it and inhaled hard.

"I love you too, but I'll fight you if you start acting dumb. Can't no nigga come in between me and you. bitch, and if you say different then I'mma drag you like I did that white bitch, Erin Han, freshman year."

"Damn, Ty, not like that! You beat that lying, fat, funky bitch like all your life you'd been waiting on that moment!" she said, laughing fondly at the memory.

Erin had been someone we'd considered a friend, even though we both knew that being friends with a messy hoe came with consequences. Someone always had something to say about Erin, and it was never anything good, so she stayed fighting with bitches. Sometimes, a nigga would get hit too, but that mainly happened when her personal hygiene was put on blast by whoever he was. Tesha and I had liked the fact that Erin had no issue getting with the shit because we were cut from the same cloth. It wasn't until the silly hoe thought she could talk about either of us behind our back, to some nigga who was using her toothless mouth as a dick massager, that shit changed. She didn't know her place in the world, so I had to remind her.

"I'm glad that we had this talk but don't let me have to chase after you again just to talk anymore. We're grown ass women and best friends, so you already know how I'm giving it up in the communication department," I said seriously.

"You're right, and I apologize. We've always been as thick as thieves, and our kids will be the same way, which means that I gotta get along with your baby daddy."

"Exactly. I'll be friends with your baby daddy too whenever you tell me who the fuck it is," I said, switching topics like a runner passing a baton.

"Here you go with the bullshit."

"How's that? You had the nerve to accuse me of changing up, and you really thought that I wasn't coming for the fact that you're keeping your baby daddy a secret? Be for real," I said, passing her the blunt back.

She stood there, in front of me, saying nothing as the weed burned unattended between her fingers. I was just about to tell her to quit acting funny when she shook her head like she'd made a decision.

"I don't need your judgement, Ty, and I know you well enough to know that you'll judge me for this one. I just need you to love me, sis, and if you love me, you'll leave it alone."

"I do love you, and I'll respect what you're asking, but you at least have to tell Ma who dude is," I insisted.

"Ma knows already, but she can't judge me. Not even a little bit."

Chapter 6

(David)

"I don't see any scenario where we leave Dayjah in Georgia," I said.

"Me either," Shaomi agreed.

"All I said was make it make sense to me because my great-granddaughter's life is too important to be played with."

"Ain't nobody playing, Ms. Web, because I'm prepared to kill and die when it comes to my child. I hear your concerns though, and that's why I think the safest place for her right now is with my family in Ghana," I said.

"As in Africa?" Shaomi asked, looking at me like I'd gone crazy.

Our seating positions at the dining room table allowed me to look at both women across the table from me, and right now, they wore identical expressions of doubt.

Knowing that this would go smoother if I just explained first was the reason that I opened my mouth and began speaking. Disbelief was the immediate response, which was typical, and it didn't deter me in the slightest because I offered to make a call to whoever they wanted to talk to in my family. Proving my identity was never as hard as concealing it had been these past few years, but I still offered to prove myself to either of the women in front of me.

"I can't believe that I got a baby by the future king," Shaomi said, shaking her head and smiling.

"Well, I did raise my great-granddaughter like a princess, so I'm sure she'll fit right in with her African relatives. How are you two gonna remain safe though?"

My eyes locked with Shaomi's as her mom's question sat in between us, but I didn't see the fear of the unknown that I'd expected to find. Instead, I found an extraordinary amount of determination and resolve that made her look sexy.

"We'll be fine, Ma, because we still work good together. Right, David?"

"True shit," I agreed.

"Yeah, well, just be sure not to step on your cousin's toes. You two know like I do that history repeats itself if you do nothing to change it."

"What's that supposed to mean, Ma?"

"It means don't fall for the smooth talk and promises of good dick that will change your life because you've already seen that movie. And David, don't try to remember how good the pussy is because that'll make you forget how lethal it is too. Just be good co-parents for the sake of Dayjah."

"We can do that," Shaomi said, looking at me.

I nodded in agreement, but I did have my doubts about this situation as co-parents going smoothly. Ty was rational when she wanted to be, and this definitely qualified as a situation where I needed her to be rational, but the lies would be hard to ignore. In order to protect myself from lying more, I'd simply told her that we'd talk about everything once we had time to fully discuss things. I knew the fight that was waiting for me at home, but for my daughter, I'd take it on the chin. For now, my focus was on Dayjah and making sure she remained emotionally stable and safe.

"Do you think it'll be easier to have your grandmother come with us to the Georgia state line for Dayjah's sake?" I asked.

"That won't be necessary. Your daughter is more than comfortable with you both, so I'm gonna go say goodbye to her now and help her pack some of her stuff. I expect to see her again sooner than later though, which means you two better get your shit together sooner than later. As for you, David, you may be a king in some far-off land, but this is Georgia here, sweetheart, and we don't play games in this part of the south. I know my granddaughter loves her cousin, Tynesha, but I'll choose my granddaughter all day, so that means the fact that you're with Ty now won't stop me from killing you if you don't act right. Understand?"

"I understand perfectly, and no matter what happens, I promise to treat Shaomi and Dayjah with the love, loyalty, and respect they deserve," I replied.

I didn't flinch under the older woman's intense scrutiny, and I was rewarded with a smile for that.

"Sha, I believe everything that you ever told me about this young man, so I'mma give you some good free game. Keep your panties on tight and watch Tesha and Tonya. If they ain't fucked him yet, then best believe that his pretty brown ass is on the menu."

I could feel my mouth hanging open as Shaomi laughed loudly, and her grandmother just politely got up from the table as if she didn't have all my bullshit figured out. I felt exposed and more than a little vulnerable, but I hid it well.

"Your grandmom is something else," I said once I was sure that we were alone together.

"You have no idea, but she's a great woman that I've learned a lot from. I never lied to her about who Dayjah's dad was, and believe it or not, she's always liked you."

"So then why did she let you keep Dayjah a secret from me?" I asked, trying to keep my tone civil.

"Because she wanted me to learn how to be a mother on my own in case you never wanted to be a father. It wasn't personal. It was about survival for me and Dayjah."

Of course I wanted to argue until I was blue in the face, but not a word I said would get me a second that I missed from Dayjah's life. As for Shaomi's grandmother, I knew that she lived by the saying 'mama's baby, daddy's maybe,' so she'd done what any strong, Black woman had done before her. She'd showed her granddaughter and great-granddaughter how to be strong, Black women, and I could only be grateful for that because the world needed more of them to celebrate. It was time that I did my part now, and I was up to the challenge.

"Are you ready for the drama?" I asked, looking her squarely in the eyes.

"I don't know. Am I? What secrets are you hiding?"

"And why would I even think to answer that question?" I asked, smirking.

"Because I can't avoid certain things or topics if I don't know what needs avoiding so let me know where the bodies are buried."

"You know, there was a point in time when I wouldn't have hesitated or thought twice about spilling my deepest, darkest secrets to you. The girl I used to know would just keep them safe. Now, I know that you love someone more than me, which means that she gets your unconditional loyalty, and I'm understanding of that. So, I've gotta keep my own secrets this time around in order to keep us all safe, and all I need from you is for you to carry yourself like you're above the bullshit. Your walking into an ordinarily hostile environment just because of these women's personalities, but now, you gotta factor in the betrayal they'll feel coupled with the fact that they're pregnant... You're basically putting a loaded gun without a safety to your temple and playing with the trigger," I stated, offering up some brutal honesty.

"I ain't scared of none of them, and every woman in this equation knows that betrayal is a two-way street. You're my baby daddy, and what that means is no matter how bad Ty may wish it, she can't kick your dick out of my past. I know the same thing about you and her pussy because she's carrying your kid. I'm not tripping, and all I request is that everyone play their position. Including you."

"What does that mean, Sha Sha? What's my position?" I asked, smiling.

"I know that you better take that mufuckin sexiness out of your tone before I put this pussy on your face right now," she suddenly growled with breathless hunger.

My smile vanished, and the hair on my knuckles stood up, searching the air for electrical current.

"What makes you think I'll let you put your pussy on my face?"

"Tell me that I can't... and watch what I do next," she threatened, seductively moving closer to me.

I felt the involuntary movement of my tongue darting in between my lips to taste the air for the enemy's scent as my body's temperature continued to rise.

"Dangerous games, Sha Sha."

"Just admit that you're scared to play," she whispered, smiling.

"Shaomi, come help us," her grandmother demanded.

The voice sounded far away, but the brief break in conversation let me know that Shaomi's grandmother was actually standing next to us. I had no idea when she'd walked up, and I doubted Shaomi knew either.

"To be continued..."

"If you can handle it," Shaomi said under her breath as she stood up.

Her grandmother pushed her in the direction of Dayjah's room while saying something that I couldn't overhear, but I heard Shaomi giggling. I took two deep breaths before pushing what had happened from my mind and pulling out my phone. I had a few missed calls from Tesha but more from Tynesha than anyone else. I hadn't been ignoring her completely, but I'd kept shit short and to the point. I knew that she was hurt, and she was trying not to lash out at me because it wasn't like this was my fault. I knew that we'd have to deal with this together though, but it couldn't begin to happen until we were physically breathing the same air once again. The message that I sent her let her know that our time to talk was close because we were headed home shortly. She hit me right back with a message that was a video link, and I curiously clicked it open. Immediately, a video began playing of her sitting outside at night with a flashlight pointing at the words *Next Generation* glowing in ink across her stomach while she sang along to music playing in the background. The song playing was by Moneybagg Yo, and its title was *Time Today*. The video ran for about thirty seconds total and ended with Ty rapping into the screen like she was the real creative force behind the lyrics.

"I don't like niggas. I don't like bitches. I don't like nobody! We can get gangsta. We can keep it cordial. How you wanna go bout it? I don't back track. Man, fuck that. I don't miss nobody. Left it on seen. I ain't write back. I don't trust nobody!"

From there, the screen went black, and then, I heard an eerie evil laugh meant to invoke a feeling one would describe as sinister. I had no idea what the hell would make Ty shoot this, but the message she was sending was a clear one. She was on all bullshit! If I'd simply stumbled across the video, then I'd probably feel like I could talk some sense into her, but being that she intentionally sent it to me, I knew my words would fall on deaf ears. I'd made her feel alone by refusing to speak about what was going on in Georgia, and now, she felt that she was on her own. I pushed back against that idea in her head immediately by sending her a text telling her how much I loved her and needed her. Then, I sent her video to my aunt and uncle in Africa, explaining my last forty-eight hours and asking for their help to keep my growing family safe. Uncle Umar responded for both of them within seconds, leaving a smile on my face with this three-word problem solving.

"On our way," I read aloud.

I didn't tell Ty that her In-laws were on the way, but I did tell her to take the video down from wherever she'd posted it because it could send the wrong message. I made sure to remind her that I was on my way home, and we would talk as soon as I got there because I needed my best friend. I could only hope that she still felt like that was her.

"Daddy, I'm ready!" Dayjah squealed, running into the kitchen and flinging her little body into mine.

I caught her but only because I dropped my phone immediately. It was worth it to see that smile transform and light up her gorgeous face.

"Let's get your stuff and put it in my car," I suggested.

Dayjah led me by the hand to her three suitcases sitting by her bedroom door, which I grabbed to take outside.

"Wait right here, sweetie," I said once I had the front door open.

Out of reflex, I scanned the street for any threat, and even though I didn't see or feel anything out of place, I still insisted that Dayjah wait at the door for me. In under thirty seconds, I had her luggage secured in the car, and we were walking back into the kitchen.

"Dayjah, say goodbye to your great grandma again because we're getting ready to leave," Shaomi said.

Dayjah ran to her great grandma, but my eyes were on Shaomi, who was moving toward me with my phone in her hand.

"I dropped that," I said lamely, holding out my hand for it, while holding my breath.

"I noticed... and I looked at the video too."

I would've cussed her out for being nosy, but what did it really matter? I slipped the phone in my pocket and focused on the drive in front of us because it was sure to be a long one, at six to eight hours depending on traffic, and neither of us had had any sleep last night. It seemed crazy to make the run back to Florida so soon, but I felt unsafe, and the longer that feeling persisted, the more harm it did mentally. It was time to go.

"I'll meet you two in the car," I said, heading back outside.

Five minutes later, I was behind the wheel of my Dodge Hellcat, headed southeast doing ninety miles per hour. My body was fatigued, but my mind was the definition of razor-sharp precision.

"We good?" Shaomi asked.

My eyes stayed on the rearview mirror, looking backwards into the past that none of us could seem to outrun.

"Yeah, we're good, but they're still back there. Same black, four door sedan that followed us from my apartment building in Florida when we'd left."

"Do you think they're gonna make a move on us now that we're headed back?" she asked.

"I'm almost positive they will."

"So, what do we do?" she asked, looking into the backseat at our blissfully innocent daughter.

"We're gonna have to make our move first."

Chapter 7

(Tynesha)

"Ty?"

"I'm in the bathroom, Ma."

I heard her footsteps approaching the door I was behind, and then, I saw the knob turn.

"You shitting?"

"Nah, nosy old lady. I'm taking a soak in this jacuzzi tub to calm my nerves," I admitted, reaching for the half smoked blunt in the ashtray and relighting it.

"Damn, your bathroom is like the size of a bedroom downstairs! I see now why you insisted on moving up here, oh great Queen Tynesha, wife of the Almighty King David."

"If you don't cut out the simple shit," I replied, laughing.

"Seriously though, I did come to speak with you about the current living arrangement."

"What's wrong with the living situation?" I asked, motioning for her to take a seat on the side of the jacuzzi.

I passed her the blunt and let her expand her lungs before she explained what was on her mind.

"You said that David texted you and said that they were coming back, and Dayjah is with them?"

"Yeah, that's what he said," I replied, trying to sound nonchalant even though my heart was beating faster.

"And where are they staying?"

I'd already followed my mom's train of thought, but the truth was that I didn't have an answer to the problems Dayjah's presence presented.

"It's okay if you don't know how to navigate this, sweetheart, and you should already know that I'm right here with you," she said, passing me the blunt back.

"What would you do if you were in my position, Ma?"

The way she immediately started choking almost made me drop the blunt in the water, but she quickly raised her hands and stood up to counteract the coughing.

"You good?" I asked, trying to suppress my laughter bubbling up.

"Y-Yeah, I'm straight, but damn, that shit burned. I'm talking about the thought of being where you are in life, not the weed smoke."

"I get it," I replied in a deadpan voice meant to convey my slightly hurt feelings.

"On some real shit though, sweetheart, I don't know what I would do in your situation. I've seen you with David, and I know that your love for him is different, so it's worth enduring the struggles that life with throw at you both in order to maintain that. Perfect, he'll never be, but if I had a baby by that nigga, I'd keep him locked in for life. I'm telling you this so that you can really understand that man's worth in terms of the love, loyalty, and security he provides. I also want you to be able to see him from your cousin's perspective because I'd bet my life that David is looking like a whole meal to her right now. She's way past giving two fucks when it comes to caring about the girl code because she's a permanent fixture in his life now. That means her only goal is taking that number one spot. Think about it. Would you rather live in the building or own it?" she asked logically.

We both knew what the answer was without having to speak the words, so the only obstacle was me getting over the fact that the woman we were discussing was family.

"She's my cousin though."

Yeah, and I'm your mama. The day that you let family familiarity excuse the crossing of boundaries between a man and a woman is the day you lose yourself to the game," she stated candidly.

My mother had always kept shit a buck when it came to me and Tesha because she would never allow it to be said that she didn't give her girls the game. Even with the both of us on the verge of being young mothers, our mom wouldn't say that we were victims of the game playing us because we both knew to adjust. As long as there was time on the clock then a bitch like me could get my shot off.

"So, tell me your next move, Tynesha."

"Keep my nigga close and my cousin closer."

"Does that mean you want them to stay up here with you?" she asked.

"Absolutely. I expect David to want to get to know his daughter, which means spending as much time with her as possible. Naturally, this puts Shaomi in prime position to receive his attention too, but I'mma counter that shit by explaining to Dayjah that she's a big sister. I plan to include Dayjah in my pregnancy like any great stepmother would."

The smile that I flashed my mom was genuine because I was looking forward to what was coming, and the smile she gave in return was just as genuine. The only difference was that her smile was sinister, and I understood why. This was warfare, and if I didn't mentally acknowledge that then I was destined to be emotionally fucked up.

"You know that Shaomi is gonna try to undermine you whenever she can, right?"

"Of course, and she's a worthy adversary because she knows me and David. She doesn't know us TOGETHER though, so she has no idea how hard I'mma go to keep my husband and my family. She doesn't know that him and I are solid beneath the surface," I replied confidently.

"Okay, well, it sounds like you got a game plan. Me and your sister can move up here so that you all have more room, and Dayjah will have her own room."

"Mom, that's sweet of you to volunteer like that... And I know deep down this ain't about this place being nicer than the one on the first floor," I said, giggling as I hit the blunt again.

"Fuck you, Tynesha."

We shared a laugh, along with the rest of the blunt, and then I was left alone to soak. I stayed submerged under the warm bubbles while allowing my mind room to really analyze the big picture that made up my life. Life was complicated enough before I found out I was a step mommy because my husband was wanted for capital murder, and my twin was wanted for first degree murder. The cops couldn't come on the property owned by this apartment complex but hiding in plain sight for the rest of our lives wasn't going to work. When I got out of the tub, I threw on a soft, blue bathrobe and grabbed my phone so that I could hit up my girl, Carrie. My bitch had the inside track to the legal system because she worked for a law firm and because she was that dangerous combination of beauty with brains. She'd talked fast and got David out on bond the first time he'd got jammed up by my ex, so I knew she would still be in touch with the cops in some way. Being a sexy ass, white girl had its advantages, so I hit her up and had her use them to try and get the autopsy report on Roland's bitch ass. Not only did I want to make sure that the muthafucka was actually dead, but I also wanted to know one way or another if David had been the one to kill him. I wasn't about to take the cops' word for shit, especially given how much they hated my husband. It would be child's play for the crooked ass cops to frame him for someone else killing Roland, and that was what we couldn't have happen. While waiting on Carrie to hit me back with an update, I got dressed in some black jeans and a white T-shirt, and then, I sat down at the kitchen table to do my duties as a wife and mother. I didn't know what all Shaomi and David were bringing with Dayjah, so I ordered everything from food, to clothes, and toys. No doubt she was used to running around and playing outside, so being stuck inside this castle was definitely going to require an adjustment from everyone. When my mini shopping spree was done, I turned my attention to dinner, but a text from David told me that they wouldn't arrive until sometime after 4 a.m. Somehow hearing this zapped my energy and put me in a foul mood, so I decided to just watch movies and smoke more weed. I shot an open invitation to my mom and sister but only Tesha came upstairs.

"What we watching?" she asked as soon as I opened the door.

"Michael B. Jordan, with his sexy ass, in *Creed*. I figured that we can start with the first one and work our way through the series."

"That's a plan, bitch!" she said, closing the door behind her and following me.

After a brief detour to the kitchen to grab some snacks and sodas, we headed to the living room and let *Creed* dominate the surround sound. We were about an hour in when I paused the movie and turned to my twin.

"Is it crazy that I'm debating whether or not to kill her?" I asked seriously.

"If it's crazy, then I'm right in that car with you, sis. Don't get me wrong. I love Shaomi, and I know she was more like a sister than a cousin, but right now, she just seems like..."

"An opp," I finished, knowing how crazy that shit sounded.

"That's exactly how I'm feeling, like she's the opps, and she wants all the things that she didn't earn yet."

"I know that you're vibe is because you're feeling mine, but I'm not intentionally trying to look at her with the side eye," I said.

"I understand that... but you are contemplating killing her, ain't you?"

Her question should've left me feeling shocked and appalled because this was my blood family we were discussing. The truth prevented me from saying a word though, and I knew that the look exchanged between Tesha and I was enough said.

"I'm not gonna involve you in my bullshit like you're not pregnant with your own issues," I said.

"We've got the same problems regardless, and you know that I'm with you whether you ask me to be or not."

"Then help me keep my mind off of killing Shaomi and let's figure out what we're gonna do about life," I insisted.

"Well, I've been thinking about my whole situation with Darryl, the governor's son, and I think that my best bet is to turn myself in. Just having my prints on a gun doesn't automatically convict me because the big question is why did Roland have that gun in his possession? With him dead and unable to give his excuses, I think it's best for me to go on the offensive."

"I can see the advantages to that strategy, but we gotta be prepared for Zoe Pound wanting to silence you for shining a light that touches their shadows," I stated seriously.

"Based on what me, you, and David did, I'd say that it's a safe bet that Zoe Pound ain't about to forgive or forget. So, there's no point in giving a fuck or playing nice with them but contacting Darryl's dad could save me now."

"Do you think that the governor will be willing to hear you out at least?" I asked curiously.

"I think he will because he's still very much in the public eye, and he doesn't want his son's skeletons to be the albatross around his own neck. The parent in him wants justice, but the politician in him knows that the levee holding the flood back is fragile at best. Darryl was never squeaky clean, and I know for a fact that his daddy had to buy silence before."

"I support your decision, and I'll talk to him for you, just to get a feel for his true intentions," I volunteered.

"It's amazing to me that we can still pull the switch without anyone knowing the difference. Shit, David probably wouldn't know the difference either."

"Oh, he would definitely know that you're not me, and I wouldn't play like that with him anyway," I replied, dismissing the idea of mentally fucking with my husband.

Every one of us was wound too tight to play games because every move was life or death at this point.

"We'll make the call later today after David is back with Dayjah and Shaomi. You good with that?" I asked.

"That's cool."

I raised the remote with the intentions of resuming the movie, but my phone started singing Trey Songz from the other room. I dropped the remote and leaped up off the couch at a dead run, heading for our bedroom where I'd left my phone charging. It was glowing green on the nightstand, beckoning me to it, and I hurried to catch the call before I missed it.

"Hey, baby," I said, smiling widely because this was the first video call I'd received since he left.

I saw David's mouth moving, but I couldn't hear a word he was saying over the roar of the 392 Hemi engine under his hood, screaming as it ate through its gears. The look on his face said it all though, and I felt my stomach drop because I couldn't think of one thing in this world that would frighten my husband.

"Bae, what's wrong?" I asked, scanning the video while trying to commit everything important to memory.

"...chasing us..." he said.

"Where are you, David?"

"...chasing us. Ten minutes out... Light the parking lot up," he said.

My mind rattled while trying to put together what he said versus what he meant, and I felt fear gripping me tighter because I knew this was the one moment where I couldn't misunderstand.

"I'll be ready," I replied.

His brief smile let me know that I did, in fact, understand what he was trying to communicate. The screen went black in my hand, causing me to fight with all my will not to scream.

"Tesha!"

Within seconds, I heard her running toward my room, but I was already headed toward the weapons we would need.

"What's wrong, Ty?"

"I don't know, but we gotta be ready because David is being chased," I said, rapidly punching in the safe's combination.

"Ready for what? What does he need us to do?"

"Save them. We gotta save them," I replied shakily.

Chapter 8

(David)

"David, tell me that you have a plan," Shaomi said, hanging on as we slid sideways around the off ramp for an exit.

I barely kept the paint on the driver's side of my car, but that reality didn't force me to ease up on the gas even a little. I made the pedal touch the floor as soon as I spotted another straightaway for us to race down. I'd thought I had them outrun in Georgia when I'd lost the car that had been following us since we'd left Florida, but I'd never been more wrong. Whoever it was that was hiding behind the tinted windows had called ahead, replacing the four-door sedan with a white, two-door Dodge Challenger that was capable of keeping up with my Hellcat. Knowing that my daughter was in the backseat meant that I couldn't afford to play defense, which was why my Sig Sauer P290 .223 was kicking and screaming out the window from the jump. My only plan after that was to keep shooting.

"We're almost home," I said, swerving around a slow-moving SUV.

I heard slugs slam into the trunk of my car, forcing me to immediately reach my hand behind the seat in a blind search for Dayjah.

"Dayjah?! Baby, are you okay?"

"D-Daddy!" she cried, grabbing onto my arm frantically.

"Just stay down, sweetheart!" I yelled, pulling my arm back so that I had both hands to control the steering wheel.

"I got her, just keep it steady for a few seconds," Shaomi said, climbing from the passenger seat to the back.

This was one of those times in life when I was so glad that Shaomi was tiny because she was able to get her and

Dayjah on the floor and wrap herself around our daughter. Shaomi wasn't bulletproof, but she was definitely willing to sacrifice herself to keep Dayjah safe.

"Stay down. We're almost there," I said, pulling out my phone and dialing blindly.

The feelings of relief that flooded my nervous system when I heard Ty's voice and saw her face were short lived but greatly felt.

"Ty, we've got shooters chasing us. Can you hear me?"

"Where are you, David?" Ty asked.

The light in her green eyes was shining in a way that was both frantic and attentive, which meant that even if she couldn't hear me, she'd still hopefully understand.

"Ty, listen. Someone is chasing us, and we're like ten minutes out from the building. Be in the parking lot and light that muthafucka up. Can you hear me, bae? Light the parking lot up," I demanded desperately.

I couldn't tell if she understood what I was saying, but I could see her beautiful mind working with the speed of an avalanche.

"I'll be ready," she replied.

My smile was one of relief, but the sound of a fast-approaching V8 engine directed my attention to the rearview mirror.

"Hang on!" I yelled, seconds before the white Dodge Challenger slammed into us from behind.

I was coming up fast on a four-way intersection, and the hit we'd taken had my car in a wild spin to the right. Trying to turn out of it would more than likely get us T-boned by another vehicle, so I did the opposite of my reflexes and turned into the spin. By the time I'd reached the middle of the intersection, I'd pulled a complete 360, and I was back in control of the speeding Hellcat. I was only a few blocks from my building, but I knew that I needed to give Ty enough time to get the Mossberg grenade launcher out and get downstairs.

I'd been trying to get a good look at who was chasing and shooting at us, but the darkness was their friend for now. All that I knew for sure was that the two niggas I'd seen looked like the same niggas from the parking lot the day my car had been blown sky high. Coincidence didn't even cross my mind and neither did avoiding the bigger problem that this signified. I took the longer way to get to my safe haven of diplomatic immunity, but I immediately spotted two black SUVs blocking the entrance to my apartment complex. Six men with guns gripped in their hands were standing and leaning by the SUVs, like they were bored. I fumbled around on the front seat for my phone until I had it in my grip, quickly hitting the buttons to connect the last number I'd called. When Tynesha didn't answer, I felt panic cascade from the roots of my hair down to my toenails, but before I could call her back, everything changed. Suddenly, the pitch-black night resembled the sunrise out over the ocean on a crisp east coast morning, and this was due to the first SUV exploding. The second one ignited as fast as the first one had, sending twisted metal and disintegrating fiber glass airborne just in time for me to drive through it.

"Get ready to run," I said, aiming the car straight at the fast-approaching high rise in the distance.

I could've simply pulled into the underground garage safely, but I knew that my wife was laying covert fire out there in the dark. There was no way I'd leave her. I yanked on the emergency break while spinning the steering wheel to the left, causing my car to do a smokey 180° turn and stop.

"Run!" I yelled, hopping out with the P290 in my grip.

"David!" Ty yelled.

My head swiveled left in time to see the white Dodge Challenger getting ready to make Tynesha a life-sized hood ornament.

"Duck!" I ordered, raising my gun and letting my finger dance on the trigger like a stripper twerkin for tuition.

The windshield blew inward, and red mist flew, but the car swerved wildly and ran into a parked car. My gun swung from side to side as I advanced on Ty, looking for any and all threats.

"David!" Tesha called, popping up from behind a car, holding a 9mm Berretta while moving in my direction.

"Where's Tonya?" I asked.

"On the balcony with the .308 sniper rifle," Ty replied.

"Everybody inside now," I instructed, keeping my eyes on the parking lot while backing up toward the building.

I could hear the sound of rescue engines in the distance, but anyone littering the asphalt had firmly given up breathing as a hobby. It only took a few minutes for all of us to be secured inside the apartment building, and Ty led the way into our first-floor apartment. Once we were inside with the door locked, I immediately went to Dayjah and checked her from head to toe. The way her entire body was trembling reminded me of a frightened puppy, and that made me homicidal mad.

"It's okay, baby. You're okay," I assured her over and over, trying to soothe her as she clung to her mom.

I motioned for Shaomi to follow me, and I led them to a back bedroom where it was quiet.

"Dayjah, you're safe, honey. I promise. I want you to stay in here with your mommy and try to go back to sleep."

"No, Daddy, wait! Don't go," she pleaded, reaching out her hand for me.

"I'm here, baby. I'm not leaving," I said softly, taking her from her mom's arms and carrying her to the bed.

I laid down with her, and Shaomi laid down on the other side of her. I was stroking Dayjah's hair while Shaomi held her hand, and eventually, she was able to doze off. Slowly and carefully, we extracted ourselves from the bed, careful not to wake her up, and then, we just stood there for a moment, watching her sleep. I felt something in my chest that was completely foreign to me because it felt like peace, and I'd never known that before. I felt eyes on me, and when I looked up, I saw Ty standing in the doorway with a guarded expression masking her facial features. Shaomi tried to take my hand in hers, like she didn't know her cousin was standing right there, but I shook her off and went out into the hallway.

"Thank you, baby. For real. Thank you," I said, pulling Ty into my arms and holding her tight.

"No problem but you owe me an extra date night this week," she mumbled into my chest.

She tried to sound nonchalant, but the shaking in her body was betraying her right now. I held her to me, keeping her secret and allowing her to regroup by finding her grounding in me. It was these moments when the magnitude of our love made everything else make sense, and fear had no control whatsoever. I'd known love before, but I'd never known all that came with love this unconditional in every sense of the word. I filed this moment away in my memory, knowing that it would keep me at one hundred percent in the long days to come. As much as I loved Ty and I craved being around her, I could not and would not continue to allow her and our child to be put at risk. As a man, I would lay down my life for my wife and kids, but I refused to let her lay down hers.

"Where is your mom and sister?" I asked.

"Waiting on us in the living room."

Ty's hand slid comfortably into mine as she led the way to the living room. I could feel Shaomi's presence as she followed us back up the hallway, but I was wondering what the fuck was going on in her mind. I hadn't meant my actions to be cold or callous toward her when she'd tried to take my hand in hers, but she had to know that her timing was terrible. Even if my wife hadn't been standing there watching us, it was still a bad idea to get physically close like that after such an emotionally charged situation. If there was time to explain later on, then I would, but right now, I had more important shit to handle.

"Okay, I need all of you to listen up because I'm only gonna say this once. Tynesha, Tesha, and Tonya, I'm putting you three on a plane with Dayjah, and you're going to Ghana. My aunt and uncle will be here soon, and you'll travel back with them. Shaomi and I will stay here until we make sure it's safe for you all to come back."

"And what happens if you die?" Ty asked calmly.

"Then you stay in Africa and raise our kids," I replied.

"You can't ask us to do that, David. You can't ask us to tuck tail and run like some scared bitches because we weren't raised like that," Tesha said.

"Facts," Tonya chimed in.

"Right now, I don't care how you were raised because the only thing that matters is the future of the kids you're carrying. They don't get to choose to be gangsters, and I'm damn sure not letting any of you decide that for them. You're leaving town immediately, but the choice is yours in whether you fly first class or with the cargo," I said seriously.

Before anyone could say anything else, the phone started ringing, freezing us all. At first, I just stood there, waiting on someone to answer it, but then, I realized that it was the landline in my apartment. I grabbed the cordless off of the side table and answered.

"Uh, hello?"

"David, its Umar."

"Yes, Uncle. I was just about to call you and tell you what happened at..."

"I know what happened, David. I was there," he said softly.

My eyes suddenly darted around the room as if I expected him and my aunt to pop out like we were playing hide and seek. It only took a few seconds for me to realize how silly that seemed.

"Uncle, if you were here, then where are you now?"

"I'm at the hospital. It's-It's your aunt. She was shot somehow during the mayhem."

"Is-Is my auntie gonna be..."

"No... no, she's not. Your aunt is dead, David. She died in my arms."

Chapter 9

(Tynesha)

I couldn't hear the other side of the conversation that David was having, but the sudden pressure that I felt from him squeezing my hand said a lot. I could feel him trembling through his fingertips, and it sent chills up my spine. I locked eyes with my twin and my mom, giving them a subtle movement of my head to let them know that shit had gone from bad to worse. David might not have known his aunt and uncle long, but I'd seen them all together, and I knew how much they loved each other. The thought of something happening to either of them put a lump in my own throat that made it difficult to swallow.

"I understand, Uncle... I will see you soon," he replied, hanging up the phone.

When he lowered the phone from his ear, I looked up into his eyes and witnessed his pain magnify as the tears built. I put the phone back in the charger and pulled him into my arms without a word. Tesha, our mom, and Shaomi all gathered around us, laying a comforting hand on his back so that he could feel the love and support surrounding him. David was one of the strongest men I'd ever known, but I could feel the stresses weighing him down, and it was enough to have me worried.

"Baby, if you want me to go, I will, but I truly don't want to leave your side," I said, bracing my hands on his chest and looking up into his face.

The sadness in his eyes was fit for a man three times his age that had lived a long life of losing people, and it hurt my heart. I knew that he needed me because I could see that vulnerable little boy in him that he'd fought hard to hide. Leaving him was the absolute last thing that I wanted to do, but I'd do what he told me.

"I can't... I can't protect you here. I can't protect any of you," he confessed painfully.

"Nobody said that you had to protect us or carry this burden by yourself, David. This is what family is for," Tesha said.

"She's right. Plus, we ain't some weak wallflower ass bitches, pregnant or not," Shaomi stated.

David wasn't verbally responding, but I could see all of these facts being spit being factored into whatever move he was contemplating next.

"This shit is about to become way more volatile and dangerous," he said with a renewed strength in his voice.

"What do you mean?" I asked.

"My aunt was killed tonight by whoever was gunning for me, and my uncle is not the type to take this lying down. He's a man of pride and a man of action who has a lot of influence."

"Not to be funny or anything, but doesn't his influence stop in Africa?" my mom asked.

David's response was a humorless laugh that was as eerie as it was unexpected.

"My uncle is a renowned businessman, and he's respected as such, but he's also feared by a lot of people because of things that he's done. Those things may have been done in Africa, but I can promise you that the location isn't important for a man as disciplined and principled."

"So, are you saying that your uncle is about to get with the shit out here in these streets?" I asked.

"His army is on the way as we speak," David replied.

"His... army?" Tesha asked, looking confused and intrigued at the same time.

"Yes, his private army. These are men who are currently in the armed services, or are former mercenaries, that are on the payroll of my family in Ghana. It's not uncommon for things to be like this, especially with those of a Royal bloodline. The problem is that the things that are acceptable in other countries would be considered war crimes in the United States, and my uncle doesn't care."

"Would you care if you were in his shoes?" I asked gently.

The look he gave me answered my question with swift decisiveness, and it also told me how this situation would probably play out.

"David, we agreed to send Dayjah to Africa, and I think that still needs to happen, but maybe you need to think about taking that flight yourself," Shaomi suggested.

"That's not an option," he replied simply.

"Then we're staying here with you because leaving you to die ain't an option," Tesha said.

The firmness in her voice kind of surprised me, but I was grateful that she had my back in supporting my husband.

"I agree with my daughters, which means we need to figure out our next move," my mother said.

"I need to know who the fuck is responsible for what happened," David said.

"All I saw were muthafuckas in suits with big guns," Shaomi offered.

"Could it be the Feds?" Tesha asked.

"Nah, because them niggas went from following us to shooting at us with absolutely no in between," he replied.

"With all the different people in this building, I would think that there are cameras that captured the opps' faces. I'm sure that our wonderful neighbors would help us get a good look at them if you asked nicely," I suggested, smiling at him.

"I'll bake cookies," he replied sarcastically.

"Use a lot of weed," Shaomi recommended.

That got us all to chuckle a little and lightened the mood somewhat, but I could still see the shadows that caused a haunted look on David's face. I appreciated his beauty that showed through his agony, but I hurt for him and wished that I could take his pain away. Since that wasn't possible, I focused on what needed to be done.

"Bae, I want Dr. P. to have a look at Dayjah, just to make sure that she's okay. Are you and Shaomi good with that?" I asked.

I saw his love for me set his eyes ablaze, and it made my stomach flip in a good way.

"Dayjah is fine," Shaomi said calmly yet firmly.

The finality in her tone rubbed me the wrong way, but I didn't get a chance to say shit.

"You know what? While we're all here, let's go ahead and get shit straight," Tesha began.

"T, you don't need to..."

"Un uh, Ma, I do need to say this. Shaomi, you grew up like our sister, so the fact that you didn't tell us about a whole kid, my nigga, is fucking crazy. What's done is done though. What I'mma need you to do now though is let David be a dad and recognize that Tynesha is Dayjah's stepmom. They're married, in case you didn't know, and that's just what it is. So please understand that you don't get to shit on that just because you're baby mama number one," Tesha advised.

"First of all, I'm not trying to undermine or shit on their marriage, and I respect their decision to be together. What I need all of you to understand is that Dayjah is mine and David's daughter, so we'll make the decisions for her. Please and thank you."

My mouth flew open with wicked intentions, but then, David's lips collapsed on mine like a life raft inflating, and we were kissing. The thoughts of violence that had been screaming in my brain were drowned out by my pussy singing Jodeci songs, and I was okay with all of that. When he pulled back, I heard the growl in my throat, and I opened my eyes to the sight of my man's seductive smile.

"We've got bigger issues than fighting with each other," he said softly.

I nodded once and gathered my composure.

"Damn, I bet you can talk the hair off a bitch pussy," my mom said.

Tesha laughed out loud, and I noticed Shaomi moving away from us in the direction of the bedroom that Dayjah was in. I leaned into David and kissed him again, just to remind him that I could give as good as I could take. Then, I stepped back.

"How long before your uncle arrives?" I asked, refocusing.

"I don't know, but he's probably gonna wanna hit the ground running, so I'm gonna go see the security guys about the camera footage."

"Okay, and I'll..."

The sudden sound of an alarm blaring startled me enough to make me jump and cling to David fearfully.

"What the fuck is that?!" Tesha yelled.

I didn't have the foggiest idea, but I was watching David carefully, and the way he was looking around the apartment heightened my feelings of anxiety.

"David, what do we do?" I asked, talking loudly despite our closeness.

He held up his index finger in the gesture for me to wait a minute, and I could see his lips moving as he continued to look around. I figured out that he was counting just as he reached the number thirty, and just as suddenly, the alarm shut off without warning.

"They picked a hell of a time to do a fire drill," Tesha said.

"This ain't a drill," David replied with a faraway look in his eyes.

"Bae, what does the alarm mean? What's going on?" I asked.

I felt the ground beneath my feet tremble, and the sounds that accompanied it were that of gears turning from somewhere unseen. It felt like I was in a scene from a movie as shadows shifted and intensified until the rising sun that had been making its presence known outside vanished behind the sound of a lock clicking loudly. The air ceased moving, and the feeling that spread around the room was hard to describe, except to say that it felt like the building was holding its breath.

"D-David, what just happened?" I asked softly.

"Lockdown protocol," he replied, still looking around curiously.

"What the fuck do you mean lockdown? Explain that shit," my mom demanded, sounding slightly hysterical.

"Mom, breathe," Tesha said, recognizing the claustrophobia that we'd inherited from her.

"I'm breathing, bitch, but David better start goddamn talking."

"One of the many security features of this exclusive building is a lockdown protocol, but it's only activated during extreme situations," David explained.

"Like if the building were under attack, then it would be locked down to keep whoever out?" Tesha asked.

"Yeah, that's one way it works, but..."

"But what, David?" I asked, getting that bad feeling in my stomach again.

"The other time a lockdown is triggered is if there are opps in the building already. They're locked in so that they can't escape."

"So, that would make the building some sort of... death trap," I said, not liking the taste of the words coming out of my mouth.

"If a muthafucka is bold enough to cross into another country then you must be willing to play by their rules," he said simply.

"And what are the rules?" Tesha asked sarcastically.

"Kill or be killed," he replied, finally looking me in the eyes.

It was on the tip of my tongue to tell him to cut the bullshit, trying to scare us, but then I heard a sound that could never be mistaken for anything else right now.

"Was that a gun going off?" my mom asked.

David's response wasn't verbal. He just pulled his gun out and checked the clip.

"I want all of you to get ready to move because we can't stay here," he informed us.

"Why-why can't we stay here?" Tesha asked, suddenly not sounding too gangsta.

"Because I'm betting that whoever is in the building is going door to door so getting to my other apartment should buy us some time. It all depends on how many people are part of this attack," he replied, pulling his phone from his pocket.

"What are you doing?" I asked impatiently, pulling my own pistol out and checking my bullet count.

"Lockdown protocol makes the security footage available to me and you in real time so let's just see what we're up against."

I stepped to his side so that I could look at the phone's screen, and what I saw made my mouth go dry. The cameras outside showed the still smoldering remains of the SUVs that I'd blown up, but my eyes immediately went to the many men moving through the parking lot like a tactical unit. I counted fifteen men with guns big enough to knock a giraffe down or blow a megalodon out of the ocean. The cameras inside the building showed about half that number of men, but their guns were still big as fuck.

"They're one floor up, baby."

"That's because they would've come in through the front entrance without realizing that the first floor was one level down. They're sure to realize that mistake soon, so we gotta go. Now," he demanded, turning and hurrying toward the room where Dayjah was.

"Get ready to shoot," I said, looking at my mom and Tesha.

Both women pulled out the guns I'd equipped them with before we had to hold down the parking lot, and they followed my lead to the front door. While we waited, I pulled my phone out and synced it to the building's WiFi server. Once my print was verified, I was given access to the same things as David, and I quickly pulled up the live camera feed for the building's interior. When I saw two men entering a stairway and going down instead of up, my heart was suddenly beating in my toenails. The lighting in the hallways was almost pitch black except for when the stairway door was open, and that gave me a wild idea.

"Stay here," I whispered, slowly pulling open the front door and easing soundlessly out into the darkness. I could barely make out the Taurus G3X 9mm I had stretched out in front of me, but my hand was steady, and my grip was sure. The one thing that I kept telling myself was what David said the rules to the game were. It was kill or be killed. Before I had time to question my capabilities for close quarters contact, the stairway door opened ten feet in front of me, and I took one last deep breath. Then, I started shooting.

Chapter 10

(David)

"It's okay, sweetie. We're just going upstairs to Daddy's other apartment," I said, attempting to soothe Dayjah as she clung to me.

"Mommy."

"I'm right here, baby. It's okay," Shaomi said from behind me.

We'd just reached the living room when I heard rapid gunfire close enough to put a knot in my stomach.

"Take her and stay behind me," I said, passing Dayjah off and heading for the front door. "Where's Ty?" I asked Tesha as soon as I saw her and Tonya peeking out the front door.

"In the hall," Tesha replied.

Nothing else needed to be said because I was moving fast with my gun ready.

"Bae?" I called out.

"Two at the end of the hallway, ten feet away, with more coming from above. Get everyone on the elevator," Ty instructed, still firing shots into the darkness.

Luckily, the elevator was on the opposite end of the hallway next to another stairway, which gave us a way out. It also meant that we were moments away from being fish in a barrel for the shooting.

"I got you covered. Move to the elevator," I said, levelling my gun off and letting it sing to the darkness.

There was no sound of screams, only the thud of bodies dropping. I could feel my peoples moving behind me, but my eyes never swayed from the darkness.

"Bae, come on," Ty said.

The stairway door in front of me opened just as she beckoned me, and I got the chance to let my gun sing an encore. Within seconds, it turned into a duet, and I could feel the heat of bullets flying past me from Ty's shots at the opps.

"Ty, you gotta get on the elevator. It won't move without your prints," I reminded her.

"I'm not moving without you," she replied stubbornly, yanking on my arm hard enough to alter my shots.

The P290 in my grip was spitting .223 rounds so fast that it acted as a nightlight that aided my vision and allowed me to knock down two more men at the end of the hall. With the hallway momentarily empty, I grabbed Ty's hand and made a mad dash for the elevator. I could hear Dayjah crying, even though her mom was trying to muffle the sound with her kisses and soft soothing, but my mind was counting the elevator's occupants. I slammed my palm in the scanner to shut the door just as I heard the stairway door creaking open again. The dull thud of bullets striking the elevator doors were the last sounds we heard before we started to rise slowly through the darkness.

"Is anybody hit?" I asked, pulling Ty into my arms and inspecting her frantically.

"I'm good, bae, I'm good. Shaomi, is Dayjah good?"

"Yeah, we good. Tesha and Tonya?"

"I'm good," Tesha replied.

"I know that I pissed on myself," Tonya confessed.

"Is that what I'm smelling?" I asked, trying to lighten the mood.

"Very funny, asshole. Just get us somewhere safe before I shit in this elevator," Tonya threatened.

I heard a fake gagging sound come out of the darkness, which made us all chuckle. There truthfully wasn't a damn thing funny, but we were all so happy to be alive that laughing was almost mandatory at this point.

When the door opened on the twelfth floor, I stepped out first with my gun swaying from side to side like it was dancing with the devil.

"Come on," I ordered everyone, heading straight to my apartment and opening the door.

When everyone was inside and I had the door bolted from top to bottom, I finally exhaled a sigh of relief. I looked around to take stock of everyone, and my first thought was that we had the look of the hunted. I'd seen this look before but only when I was the one doing the hunting. This role reversal had the taste of rage stuck in my mouth like I'd forgotten to brush my tongue. When my eyes landed on my daughter, I felt my heart stop. She wasn't crying anymore, but she had a faraway, glassy look in her eyes that made me think that she might develop a twitch one day from all of this shit. I passed Ty my gun and went to Shaomi with my arms out.

"Come here, baby girl," I said softly.

Without hesitation, Dayjah came to me, and I carried her into my bedroom where we could talk a little. I sat down on the bed with her and positioned her in my lap so that we were eye level.

"I know a lot of scary stuff has happened in the last few hours, sweetheart, and Daddy is so so sorry about that. I promise that nobody is gonna hurt you though, Okay?"

"Wh-What about Mommy? Don't let Mommy get hurt either, Daddy. Please."

The words that she spoke, coupled with the vulnerability on her tiny face, threatened my tough exterior and had me wiping tears away before they could carve a path down my face.

"I'll protect Mommy too. I promise," I said softly, kissing her on the forehead and holding her close.

We stayed like that, holding each other, until I felt her little body fully relax, along with her slow and steady heartbeat. I gently laid her in my bed before walking to my closet safe to grab more ammunition. I grabbed enough bullets to reload the one hundred round drum and both thirty round clips for my P290, and I added a Glock .27 equipped with the switch and a fifty round banana clip to my jeans pocket. When I got back to the living room, I found Ty with her face in her phone, Tesha and Tonya were throwing back shots of Pepto Bismol in the kitchen, and Shaomi was standing at the balcony door like going outside was an option.

"Talk to me, Ty. What do you see?" I asked.

"They can't make it past the first floor without someone's access code, and they can't go back the way that they came, so I'd say that the panic is about to set in."

"Good, that's really good. That should give us time to come up with a plan of action," I said, taking a seat beside her on the couch.

As soon as we huddled together to look at her phone's screen, my phone started ringing, prompting me to answer it.

"Yeah?"

"David, are you okay?" Umar asked.

"Yeah, Uncle, we're safe in the apartment upstairs. How did you know that something was wrong?"

"Because I saw the building's impenetrable dome close around it while I was in the car on the highway," he replied.

"There are men outside and some inside too. I count six men heavily armed trapped on the first floor unable to get out or move from their current position. It's a waiting game at this point."

"Yes, it is, but the clock doesn't work in your favor either. That building holds many secrets held by some very bad people, and in the unlikely event that it was ever invaded to expose or compromise those secrets, the building will cannibalize itself," he explained.

In the time that I'd known my Uncle Umar, I'd never known him to show a flair for embellishments nor understating. That meant, as crazy as his words sounded, they were undoubtedly true. I could feel the weight of just what that meant as I looked around the room at the women who were trapped with me, knowing that my unborn children were still in a life-threatening situation.

"Uncle Umar, please tell me that there's a way to prevent this. My children are in the building with me."

"Y-Your children? David, what are you talking about?"

"Look, I can explain all of that later, but I need you to tell me how to protect my family," I replied desperately.

"Once the threat is eliminated, then the self-destruct sequence will be terminated. You can't focus on the men outside because they don't pose the threat. It's the men who are in the building that you need to get to."

"Okay, and how the hell do I do that because I ain't the James Bond type," I said with growing frustration.

"I understand, David, and I promise to do all that I can to help. Let me call you right back."

Before I could respond, the line went dead in my ear, which only pissed me off more.

"Fuck!" I growled under my breath.

"That doesn't sound good, bae... Talk to me," Ty said, moving closer to me so that no one else could hear us speaking.

"There's no need to speak about it until I know for sure, so we'll wait until my uncle calls back."

"The way it sounded on this end, I'm guessing that we're not as safe as you initially thought we would be here. So, what's our plan for getting out?" she asked.

"I don't know yet, but the way my uncle is talking, we'll have to go back downstairs and kill those remaining six men or..."

"Or what, David?"

I looked her in the eyes, not wanting to verbalize the words running around in my brain but unwilling to lie to her.

"Is there any other way for us to get out of the building?" she asked.

"That's another question that I don't have the answer to, but I say that we be ready just in case. I've got enough ammo for my gun, but you need to go to the safe and get bullets for the rest of you. Do it quietly because Dayjah is asleep in our bed."

"Of course she's sleep in our bed, you big softie. I always knew that you'd be a girl dad, so I'm praying to give you lots of little girls to dote over," she said, handing me my gun and smiling as she stood up and walked off.

Having a houseful of little women wasn't even something that I wanted to joke about, but I knew that I'd love my kids no matter what. That love was the motivational factor to figure a way out of this situation, even if that meant more killing. I quickly reloaded the drum on my gun and the spare clips I had before going back to my phone to check on the unwanted guests downstairs. I didn't get to pull the live feed up though because my phone started ringing, forcing me to answer it immediately.

"I'm here, Uncle. What's up?"

"I've got good news for you, David. The committee has convened, and I was able to get them to understand that the invasion isn't about anything, or anyone, in that building except for you. For that reason, they've ruled the self-destruct protocol unnecessary, and it's been deactivated."

"That's great news. Thank you," I said, breathing a much-needed sigh of relief.

"There's a catch though. Whoever or whatever it is that followed you home must be dealt with asap because you won't get a second chance with the committee. You won't just be evicted. You and your family will be hunted and erased without warning, and there's nothing I can do about it either. Do you understand?"

"Yeah, I get it," I replied, trying not to feel some type of way.

"I know that it sounds harsh, but you must remember the type of people who live there and what their privacy is worth to them. We can't change them, but we can focus on the bigger problem now. My men are still on route, and they are prepared to wage an all our war with whoever is responsible for your aunt's death. So, David, tell me who took away one of my biggest reasons for living each day?" he asked, choking up as he fought through his despair.

I felt like telling him that I honestly didn't know who'd done it would make me a failure in his eyes, and I didn't want that on top of everything else. I wouldn't lie to him either though, which left me with one option.

"I don't know who did it, Uncle Umar, so I say we kill anyone who might have done it. I say we kill them all."

Chapter 11

(Tynesha)
(One Week Later)

It was a known fact that time never passed as fast as we wanted it to, especially when we weren't doing anything to occupy that time. Laying around the apartment had made me, my mom, and Tesha lazy as fuck, and that was morphing into irritability. We'd been at each other's throats about the dumb shit more and more until David had had enough, and he'd sent them back downstairs to live. Truthfully, our living arrangement could've gone back to normal on the same day that the building had locked down. Once the private security forces that were employed by the building's housing committee had arrived on scene, order was quickly and swiftly restored, and many people chose to tuck tail and run. Still, we'd all chosen to stay in the same apartment to offer the support that a traumatized Dayjah would need. It became obvious that Dayjah was a kid who could adjust well, despite the chaos existing around her, and she was smart too. I thought that it was going to be weird between Shaomi and me now because of Dayjah, but we'd been mature enough to put the awkwardness to the side for the greater good of creating a safe space for our kids. My body was changing and growing every day, which put my own journey of motherhood into perspective and made me want that bond with my stepdaughter even more. I was ever cautious not to do too much, but Dayjah definitely knew that I was here for her. While I'd kept my focus on Dayjah, I'd watched silently from afar as my husband struggled to find his foothold on this new version of his life. David was a natural at being a dad, and that made me excited to bring our own child into the world, but the uncertainty in our lives caused me to smoke more weed than normal to counter the anxiety. I knew that we could talk about anything, but David was playing things close to the vest when it came to all the drama still going on. Tesha had told me of her plans to turn herself in, and after taking the steps that we'd outlined, it sounded like it was going to work. She was still waiting on the new lawyer to negotiate the terms though. I didn't know if the imminent threat of being a mom was stressing Tesha or if it was her legal troubles, but whatever it was had created an awkwardness between us. It wasn't anything said or done that I could really put my finger on, but shit was different, and I could feel it. I could feel it with my mom too, and it made me feel like I was going crazy with paranoia, but I didn't know why that would be the case. Maybe it was just that part of me wanted things to go back to the simplicity of what was while the rational adult in me knew that those were children's wishes. Life moved forward fast, and you either rode that train or got hit by it. Right now, I didn't know which I was doing. A sudden sharp pain in my bladder changed my thought process and had me easing out of the bed carefully so that I didn't wake David. I made it to the bathroom without spilling a drop of urine down my leg, and that made me feel somewhat accomplished as I sat on the toilet. Being pregnant and drinking plenty of fluids made for an obscene amount of bathroom breaks, but you'd be surprised what the body could endure and adapt to. Once I was done and had my hands washed, I went back into the bedroom intending to reclaim sleep because it was only 5 a.m., but in my heart, I knew that it was a lost cause. My feet carried me to the living room where I found Shaomi sitting in front of the T.V. playing Call of Duty.

"You wanna play?" she asked.

"Yeah, I'll learn you real quick."

I sat down and grabbed the other controller while she reset the game to two player mode. At first, we played in silence because the screen was muted, and we weren't talking, but I could feel the tension in the air coming from her like her lips wanted to move.

"It's been years since we did this, but I still know you. What's on your mind?" I asked, cutting my eyes in her direction.

She looked back over at me, but she didn't say anything at first. I wasn't about to force the issue. I was simply extending the offer because we were once thicker than thieves.

"This shit ain't weird to you, Ty?"

"Which part do you mean?" I asked, chuckling softly.

"I mean the part where I had a baby by your husband. I mean, how did you and David even hook up?"

Part of me had known that this conversation was as unavoidable as it was necessary, but I hadn't such a first approach. For that reason, I took a moment to gather my thoughts before speaking.

"Me and David... That was as unexpected as it can get for real because I literally bumped into him at one of the worst moments in my life. I was mentally and emotionally defeated by my ex, and I didn't know how to escape him, so I was committed to running far away. David stopped me from running just by being who he was. Of course familiarity played a part because he was someone that I knew, but him seeing a part of me that was new and ugly, that I wasn't proud of, showed me who he really was. He didn't judge me; he didn't belittle me for not being strong enough or smart enough to leave an abusive relationship. He just helped me because that's the kind of man he is. The rest just kind of happened."

"Kind of happened? Even though the girl code says that you can't date my ex?" she asked in a tone mixed with anger and steel.

"The girl code? Shaomi, we're grown ass women so living by the girl code is not something I aspire to do. Now, the woman code is all about communication, and I would've had a conversation with you about David, but you made it clear years ago that you didn't wanna talk about him. We all understand why now, but I'm not here to judge you for that. I'm just saying that you made David fair game."

"I can admit and own the mistakes that I made with David, so I shouldn't be mad about either of your decisions to hook up and fuck. Marriage though, Ty? You actually married him knowing that he was the love of my life?"

The seriousness of the question made me pause the game and turn to face her.

"You actually left the love of your life alone for a bitch to marry?" I asked, tossing the ball back in her court.

"I was young, Tynesha, and I was pregnant by the man I dreamed of marrying, but my family wouldn't even let me entertain that idea. No one thought that David was good enough simply because they'd heard rumors about him in the streets, but I was in those streets with him. I was his ride or die, and I would've been his queen!"

"If you wanna hear God laugh then tell him what you've got planned," I replied simply.

"What the fuck is that supposed to mean?"

"It means that this thing called life is bigger than what you want because it's God's plan. If you want something bad enough though, then you don't take the first no for the final answer. You can't blame me or David for your decision to run and not fight, so I suggest you find a way to live with those demons, little cousin. He's mine now," I said, putting the controller down and standing up.

Her hand shot out and grabbed my arm, preventing me from turning and walking away.

"Don't walk away from me when we're talking."

"I said what I said, and I meant that shit, so I suggest you take your muthafuckin hand off of me," I warned, feeling the blood pumping fast in my fingertips.

"Or what, Ty? You ain't never been no fighter bitch so all that tough talking you doing don't move me," she said, standing up and getting in my face.

Her hand was on my right arm, but my left hand had already been moving to the small of my back. With everything that had been going on in our lives recently, I'd taken to keeping a pistol on me at all times. The weight of the small Glock .42 brought comfort in my hand.

"I'm only gonna say it one more time, Shaomi. Get your damn hands off me."

"Make me, hoe," she said, tightening her grip.

A dangerous glint in her eyes put no fear in my heart because I was taller, bigger, and more advanced since the last time we'd had to throw hands. I didn't feel like fighting though, and that was my justification for raising the gun swiftly and putting it to her forehead. Never in my life could I have conceived or entertained the idea of shedding the blood of my own family, but this bitch was about to be the exception.

"Mommy, will you make me and Daddy breakfast?"

At the sound of Dayjah's voice, I looked to my left and saw her standing a few feet away, rubbing sleep from her eyes with her tiny hand. Her other hand was wrapped up tightly in her daddy's, and his eyes burned brightly without a hint of sleep in them. I waited for him to say something, but he didn't. He calmly evaluated the situation and waited.

"Mommy?" Dayjah called again, forcing me to look back at Shaomi. The fire in her eyes had vanished, and all that remained was a mother's love, which softened my heart in this moment.

"We don't need to be enemies so don't take us there," I said, pulling the gun away from her head.

She didn't verbally respond; she simply moved toward her daughter and took her hand.

"Come help me make some French toast," Shaomi said, causing Dayjah to squeal with delight.

They headed in the direction of the kitchen, leaving me and David standing in the living room, looking at each other. Embarrassment quickly began to set in, causing me to tuck my pistol and cross the room to stand in front of him.

"Baby, I..."

"You don't have to explain, sweetheart. I'm surprised that it took you two this long to finally butt heads," he said, taking my hand in his and leading me back to our bedroom.

"I didn't want it to go like that though, David, because she's not just some bitch off of the streets. She's family."

"I know, but it's my fault for putting both of you in this position," he admitted.

"Babe, you can't help who you love, and it's not like you fell in love with both of us at the same time. It's definitely not all your fault either though because Shaomi made her own decisions, and she allowed decisions to be made for her. That ultimately cost you four years of your daughter's life that you can't ever get back, and that'll never be your fault."

He pulled me close to him and kissed me with a soft tenderness that made me melt at the knees. I could feel his love and devotion to me as if he was using his lips to speak the words, and I returned the message eagerly. I thought we were headed to the bed to finish what he'd started, but suddenly, he pulled back and looked down into my eyes.

"I need to tell you something."

His words and tone made my stomach drop, and I wanted to run away for reasons that I couldn't explain, but I stayed right where I was.

"You can tell me anything, baby. You know that."

"I got a message from my uncle, and it's time for us to make a few moves out here to put shit back in balance."

"Does that mean you know who's been coming at you?" I asked, dreading the answer somewhat.

"Yes and no. They're hired guns, but they didn't come cheap, and the paper trail leads back to a city councilman down in Miami."

"Miami? Who do you know down there that would wanna take a shot at you that bad to pay some hittas to move so boldly?" I asked curiously.

"The last time that I checked, I didn't have no smoke with nobody in Miami, but the councilman is Haitian so..."

"Zoe Pound," I concluded, shaking my head.

In my heart, I'd always known that all of this would come back to Roland, which meant that it was my fault. It was true that Tesha shared part of the blame for ever being in business with Roland, but it was my actions that made his psychotic ass fall in love with me. Now, even though he was dead, all of us were forced to live with the consequences of my decisions, and that didn't sit right on my soul.

"David, let me go with you. This is all because of me anyway so let me come with you and help you."

"You're cute when you're feisty, but you know damn well that I'm not letting you anywhere near the shit that's about to go down. I'll be back as soon as possible, and all I need you to do is not kill anyone here," he replied, giving me a look to convey the seriousness of his words.

"I got you, bae... Just promise to come back to us."

"Tynesha, I promise that only death could keep us apart, and that would only be until I forced the devil to kick me out of hell. It's you and me forever."

Chapter 12

(David)

Under the cover of night, I crept from the sanctuary of my apartment building out into the waiting black Lincoln Navigator idling at the side entrance.

"How are you, Uncle?" I asked, concerned by the obvious signs of lack of sleep covering his face.

"I am as well as can be expected given the circumstances."

I wanted to offer some words of comfort as we pulled off, but I knew in my heart how useless they would be if I were in his shoes. I couldn't imagine losing Tynesha, especially not to a violent death. The guilt that I felt also contributed to my inability to really offer words of comfort because I felt like my aunt had died because of me.

"What's the plan, Uncle?"

"We're headed to Miami to have a sit down."

"A sit down? Like a peace summit?" I asked in disbelief.

"Peace is needed, nephew, but peace cannot be realized without war. It does not matter who drew first blood in this war. All that matters is returning life's balance."

"And how will this meeting balance the scales?" I asked, slightly confused.

"Because the meeting is not all that is taking place right now. While we attend this sit down with Councilman Bah, his wife and family will learn the lessons of street sacrifice that they must pay. It is their blood that is the currency for peace if the councilman chooses to continue to engage in war."

I let what he'd said resonate within me as I processed what it all meant. I'd been in the streets long enough to justify shedding blood, but I'd never seen this side of my uncle before. To the world, he presented himself as a distinguished gentleman, soft spoken and intelligent, but now beneath that polish, I got to glimpse the ruthless calculation that had survived African genocide. Killing was an old sport, and it seemed that my uncle knew it well.

"What is my part in this?" I asked.

"Your presence will make it clear that we are not running. Period."

"Not to sound overly concerned, Uncle, but isn't it a little crazy to ride into this man's territory on bullshit with just me, you, and your drivers?"

"Nephew, I would never be so foolish as to walk into this situation unprepared for the immediate threat to our lives. A few of my men are tasked to detain Councilman Bah's family while the rest travel with us. You only saw me picking you up, but we're travelling in a motorcade that is fifteen SUVs strong and armed to the teeth."

His declaration made me chuckle, but I shouldn't have been surprised because my uncle was nothing if not prepared. All that was left for me to do was sit back and follow his lead. I pulled my phone out and sent Ty a text as promised so that it couldn't be said that I didn't check in with her periodically. I made sure to send a message to Shaomi for Dayjah too.

"With everything that's happened, I haven't had a chance to ask you about your daughter. How is she?"

"She's absolutely amazing. It's a completely new experience, and nothing like I've ever known, but I'm so very much in love in a different way," I replied, smiling widely.

"Fatherhood is an amazing thing, and you should cherish it always. It's a good thing that you're getting this practice too before your wife has her baby because managing two kids will be much harder."

His comment made me think, but it also made me realize that I hadn't been completely transparent with him about my kids yet.

"Uncle, I need to level with you about something. My wife's sister is pregnant too."

"Okay, well, that must be exciting for them to be pregnant at the same time, but why do you sound concerned?" he asked, looking through the shadows at me.

"Well, uh, I'm saying something about it because that baby is mine too."

I could feel his piercing stare as well as see it, and it made me feel uneasy as fuck.

"So, you're saying that you got Tynesha AND Tesha pregnant? At the same time?" he asked slowly.

"Yes."

I didn't know what to expect after I gave the simple one-word answer, but his sudden laughter wasn't it. He let out a belly rumbling laugh that filled the SUV to the point of making the windows rattle from the vibration. I didn't know how to respond, so I just sat there until he got himself under control.

"Nephew, do not think that I'm laughing at your interesting predicament. My laughter was about how this would not be so abnormal in African culture as it is to the colonized American ways of life. A man is meant to have more than one wife and to plant his seed so that his bloodline can be properly preserved. Do not fret. Just be a great dada to your kids."

"I'll try, but I can't lie. I'm scared of what will happen when my wife finds out," I confessed.

"My advice is that you don't let her find out. You tell her. She loves you, I've seen that, and you must trust that."

I knew that his advice was meant to be wisdom, but what he'd just said sounded crazy as fuck to me because telling Ty would get me killed. I understood that this wasn't a secret that could be kept forever, but there had to be a way to have the truth come out without all of the pain and suffering. Since I still had plenty of time to figure it out, I put my mind back on my present task so that my focus wasn't split. It took us a few hours to get to Miami, but there was still plenty of people out and about at 1 a.m. The meeting had been arranged for a neutral place, which was a restaurant owned by a Chinese diplomat that my uncle and Councilman Bah knew. When we pulled up, it was clear to see that there were at least ten men standing guard out front, and there was no doubt in my mind that they were armed with some heavy metal. When I pulled my gun out and chambered the first round, my uncle put his hand on my shoulder and shook his head.

"Keep your gun concealed unless the moment arises that you need to use it. There are enough guns around you to show greater force than what you see outside your window," he assured me.

I hesitated for a split second before tucking the pistol back into the waist of my pants and waited on my uncle's next move. We sat quietly for a few moments, and then, my uncle said something in an African dialect that I didn't understand, prompting the men in the front seats to get out. A few moments later, our doors were opened, and we stepped out into the humid morning air. I looked left first, and then right, finally realizing why my uncle didn't seem the slightest bit worried by the niggas we'd seen standing out front. Those men were outnumbered at least three to one by my uncle's army, and every man on our side was clutching an AK-47. I didn't understand a word of what my uncle was saying, but when he gave an order, his men formed lines that were six in front of us and four behind us. Then, we moved forward toward the restaurant. My nerves weren't rattled, but I could feel the faint flickering of butterflies created by anxiety in my stomach. I kept my eyes open because I was hyper alert, but my outward demeanor was calm as we marched past the welcome committee in front and went into the restaurant. My uncle gave a command that halted his men and let us step through the crowd so that we could continue on to the table in the middle of the restaurant's floor. The establishment was empty except for the lone occupant sitting at the table, a man of medium height and build with neatly bound dreadlocks, hazel brown eyes, and brown skin. His eyes held secrets, but he wasn't the first man I'd seen with death in him, and he wouldn't be the last. We sat down without waiting for an invitation, and the dance began.

"Councilman Bah."

"General Umar."

The councilman's eyes swung toward me, but I didn't say shit. I simply returned the stare.

"General, you asked for this meeting, so what do you want?" Bah asked.

"I wanted to offer you the chance to live to an old age or until another one of your enemies kills you. I came to offer you peace," Umar replied.

"Peace? Tell me why would I choose peace when your nephew has chosen war by interfering in my business affairs?"

"I didn't choose war. Your crooked ass cop, Roland Simms, made that choice when he refused to leave my wife and family alone," I stated calmly.

"You steal another man's woman, and you feel there will be no consequences? Just like a spoiled American," Bah said with disgust.

"Spoiled or not, this was not a war of our choosing, and that is why I'm giving you an opportunity to stop this. Now," Umar replied.

"Your words carry the tone of a threat, General, and you should be careful because I don't take kindly to threats," Bah said menacingly.

"I do not make threats, Councilman, because I'm a man of action. If you do not believe me, you're free to call your wife and daughter."

The flash of fear in Bah's eyes was instant, but it vanished just as quickly and was replaced by indecision. It was obvious to me that this man knew who my uncle was and what he was capable of because I didn't see any disbelief on his face. I saw a man stuck in between a rock and a hard place, but he didn't know it yet.

"My family has nothing to do with this," Bah said.

"You would kill another man's wife and feel there will be no consequences? Just like a dumb nigga," I said, smiling.

"I offer you a proposition, Councilman. You end the bloodshed... Or I will shed more," Umar stated calmly.

The anger in Bah's eyes was slow building, but obvious nonetheless, and seeing it made me anxious for my pistol's weight in my palm. I heeded my uncle's words though, and I didn't make any rash moves. No one spoke, which only heightened the tension in the room.

"You would kill a defenseless woman and child?" Bah asked.

"As easily as I would press a button," Umar replied, pulling a phone from his pocket.

I moved as slowly and subtly as I could until my fingers came into contact with the butt of my gun, and I was able to ease it into my right hand. The councilman's eyes were locked on my uncle's like they were engaged in an old western showdown, waiting on the clock to strike noon. There was something about the councilman's demeanor that seemed off to me though, but I couldn't quite put my finger on what it was.

"General, I am an immigrant, much like yourself, and I have seen many things that would give the average man night terrors. For you to think that you could show up and bluff me into a peace agreement is beneath your reputation. My family is always heavily guarded, and I would've been alerted if there had been any type of situation. So, if you need me to answer the question of peace or war, I choose war," Bah declared, smiling maliciously as he raised his left hand.

My eyes had been on my uncle to better gauge what the next move would be, and that was how I saw the red dot from the beam appear on his forehead. At the same time, I was conscious of the councilman's moves through my peripheral vision, so I knew that the gun in his grip was coming up on me.

Instinctively, I knew that there was no time to raise my gun, which left me with the only option of shooting under the table. I double tapped the trigger in my hand while simultaneously pushing my uncle to the left and out of the beam's glow. Everything happened within a split second, but I heard a scream of pain come from the councilman's mouth right before I got knocked sideways. It didn't immediately register to me that I'd been shot until I tried to get up, only to have the pain in my right side put me back on the ground. I heard my uncle screaming words as he grabbed my gun and fired at people that I couldn't see. Sounds of rapid gunfire reached my ears from outside, but it sounded faint. Everything sounded faint. I slowly realized that I was losing consciousness, and my last thought was of Dayjah's smile that looked so much like her mom's used to.

Chapter 13

(Tynesha)
(Next Day)

After everything that had happened with Shaomi, I knew that I wouldn't be going back to sleep for sure once David was gone. We'd played nice for the rest of yesterday, but I knew that was for David and Dayjah's sake. With him gone to handle business with his uncle, I now wondered if Shaomi was going to try to pick up where we left off, so I laid in bed, dozing lightly, with my pistol in my hand. I didn't want to kill my cousin, and once upon a time, the very idea of that wouldn't have crossed my mind, but things were different now. I was different now. I understood my responsibilities as a mother and a wife and keeping my family together was at the top of the list. As long as everyone respected that then I wouldn't be forced to use the gun gripped in my right hand right now. I laid in bed, letting my mind roam freely as the lines between conscious and subconscious blurred like I was a dope fiend nodding out. I kept seeing David's face in my mind's eye, and that brought me comfort until an unexpected bout of morning sickness sent me racing to the bathroom. I just barely got the toilet seat up before the hot bile was flying from the depths of my stomach like a reverse engineered vacuum. By the time I finished heaving, my throat was on fire, and I could feel sweat oozing from my pores. Taking a quick shower helped to balance me out a little, but when I crawled back into bed at quarter to 2 a.m., my stomach was still in knots. I prayed that nothing was wrong with David first, and then, I just laid there. I didn't know what else to do except lay a hand on my stomach and communicate with my unborn child, and that made me feel somewhat better. After another hour and a half of staring into the darkness, I gave up on sleep, got out of bed, and threw on some sweats under the big T-shirt of David's that I had on. I pulled on my Jordans, grabbed my phone, and then I was out the door, headed to the downstairs apartment. When I let myself in, I made sure to move quietly so that I wouldn't wake my mom up because Tesha was the one that I wanted to talk to. I'd just made it past the living room though when the familiar sounds of projectile vomit reached my ears, causing me to pause not far from the bathroom door. The good sister in me wanted to go in and at least hold Tesha's hair back, but I knew that any whiff of puke would reignite that same flame in me. My throat still felt raw from my own experience, so I stayed my ass right where I was. Within a few minutes, I heard the water in the sink running, which I knew signaled the passing storm and the application of soothing liquid to the mouth and throat. I leaned up against the wall, intending to scare the shit out of my twin, but when the door finally opened, it was me who got the surprise.

"Ma?"

"Dammit, Tesha, what the hell are you lurking outside the bathroom for?! You trying to give me a fucking heart attack on top of everything else?!"

"Ma, it's not Tesha," I said.

She squinted at me through the darkness before flipping on the bathroom light so that she could actually see. Not since Tesha and I were kids had our mother mixed us up, even when we'd tried to trick her, but this moment was a combination of darkness and the unexpected

"Ty-Tynesha, what are you doing down here? Is everything okay?"

"I'm fine, Ma, but the question is are YOU OKAY?"

"Oh, yeah, I'm fine, baby. I just must've ate something that didn't agree with my stomach. That's all," she explained.

If we had still been in the dark and I hadn't been able to see her face, she might have been able to slide that lie past me, but I knew her hazel green eyes like I knew my own. She was telling a bold face lie.

"Mama, how long have you known that you're pregnant? It's no use lying to me about it because it's obvious that Tesha knew what was going on when she accused you a month ago."

I could see her wheels turning as she tried to figure a way out of the truth, but I didn't understand why she wouldn't just admit it.

"Baby, it's... complicated," she replied vaguely.

"How? You're a grown ass woman, not the sixteen-year-old kid who got pregnant with twins. Your life is different now, Mama, and you can actually celebrate this pregnancy in a way that you never could when it came to me and Tesha. Unless you're not happy about being pregnant for some reason. Is that it? Do you feel like you're too old now, or do you just not want the baby?"

"No, no, that's not it. I mean, I'm only thirty-eight years old. It's just, my baby's father... he's married," she confessed.

"Oh."

I knew that the one-word response sounded lame and judgmental, but I honestly didn't know what else to say. This was the woman who taught us not to fuck, or fuck with, married men. I didn't want to throw her words back at her, which was why my response was so short.

"I know what you're thinking, Ty, but he wasn't married when we fucked, and I didn't know that he was planning to get married," she said, moving past me and heading to the couch in the living room.

I followed her and sat down beside her, taking her hand in my own to give her some comfort.

"Mama, I'm not judging you, especially because I know that sometimes shit unexpectedly happens between men and women. I just want you to know that I'm here for you too, and you can lean on me the same way that you do Tesha."

"I know that, baby, and I love you, but you should be allowed to enjoy the honeymoon phase of your relationship and the joys of being a mom for the first time," she said.

"I'm enjoying all parts of my journey, but you and my twin being pregnant at the same time as me is a new and exciting part of the journey. It's wild that it happened like that, but this can only bring us all closer."

The look of sadness in my mother's eyes didn't match her smile, but she pulled me in close for a hug before I could say anything.

"What type of hippie love and peace moment are you two having at this time of the damn morning?" Tesha asked, yawning from somewhere behind me.

My mom released me as if she was startled and caught doing something wrong, and I turned to face my twin.

"Ma finally admitted to me that she's pregnant since I caught her blowing chunks," I said, chuckling.

Tesha's eyes immediately skated past me to our mother, but there was no amusement, only questions.

"She told you that she's pregnant, huh? What else did she say?"

"What else was there to say? Unless you're talking about her baby daddy being a married man," I replied nonchalantly.

"That's what she meant," our mom said quickly.

Suddenly, I was getting a weird vibe from Tesha, like she had something that she wanted to say, but she didn't speak. Before I could question her, my phone started vibrating loud enough to make us all jump inadvertently. Somehow, I'd forgotten about David's check in call, and as I pulled my phone out, I realized that he was late, but I was still looking forward to hearing his voice.

"Hey, baby, how are..."

My question was cut off by a familiar voice that wasn't my husband, saying the three words that shattered my soul.

"David's been shot." I could still hear Umar's voice as the phone slid from my hand and bounced off of my knee.

"Ty, what's wrong?" Mom asked.

I saw Tesha pick up my phone and put it to her ear before her lips started moving. The instant trembling in Tesha's hand was immediately noticeable, and it removed all hope that what I'd heard had been a mistake or a lie.

"Oh, God," I groaned, curling up into a ball.

I could feel the warmth of tears raining down my face as the shaking in my body became more uncontrollable.

"Tesha, what's wrong?" Mom asked, more insistently than before.

"David-David got shot," Tesha replied.

Hearing her confirm what I'd heard verbally only made me cry harder as the feelings of hysteria swept through my body.

"Is he-Is he..." Mom asked, unable to even speak the word that would change my life forever.

"No, he's not dead, but he's in Miami Hospital," Tesha replied, still listening to whatever Umar was saying on the other end of the call.

I clung to the hope of David's survival like it was my life raft in the middle of the turbulent ocean. With that hope, I was able to keep myself from slipping into a catatonic state. Knowing that he was alive had my mind moving at a million miles an hour, trying to decide my next move because keeping him alive was all that mattered.

"Give me the phone," I demanded, hopping off the couch with renewed strength despite my tears steadily flowing.

Tesha complied, and I put it to my ear long enough to tell Umar that I was on my way to the hospital. I didn't know whether Tesha or our mom would try to stop me, but I didn't have the time to argue, so I simply left the apartment and hurried to the elevator. When I made it back upstairs to my apartment, I debated for a second about waking Shaomi up to tell her what happened, but I decided against it and kept moving. I quickly changed clothes and packed a small bag that included money and guns because I had no idea what I was walking into. Within a few minutes, I was back in the elevator, headed for the underground garage where David's Dodge Hellcat was parked.

David's car had definitely seen better days, and that was clear based on the missing back window and bullet holes, but it was still drivable. That was all I cared about right now. The surprise that I felt at seeing my twin and our mom leaned up against the car caused my steps to falter, but I kept moving forward.

"You're not talking me out of going so move," I said, pulling out the key fob and starting the car.

"We didn't come to talk. We're going with you," Tesha replied, opening the back door and getting in.

Our mom followed her lead by climbing into the passenger seat, and I jumped behind the wheel. Truthfully, I was glad that they were coming with me because I needed the support to prevent a mental breakdown that I felt was imminent. I used the car's GPS to map out the quickest route, and then, we were on the move. We rode in silence, but my mind was full, talking prayers and bargains with God because I'd give anything to keep my husband on this earth with me. I hadn't known the transition had been made before this moment, but now, I knew with absolute certainty that I couldn't live without my man.

"He's gonna be okay, Ty. You know David is indestructible," Tesha reassured me.

I nodded but didn't reply or take my eyes off of the road in front of me. Within two hours, I had us speeding up to Miami Hospital, and we all hit the ground at a dead run through the doors. Umar was waiting for me in the lobby, and his surprise at seeing my mom and sister was obvious.

"I don't know that the hospital staff will allow all of you in to see him at once because he is still unconscious," Umar said, looking directly at me.

"We ain't asking, so what room is he in?" Mom asked.

Umar hesitated for a moment, but then, he nodded decisively.

"Come. I will take you to him," he replied, leading the way to the elevator.

We rode in silence to the third floor, but I felt like my heart was beating hard enough to be heard over the hospital's PA system. I took several deep breaths in preparation of seeing David hurt, and when I first rounded the corner into his room, I was okay. He didn't look hurt. He simply looked like he was taking a nap. It was the sounds of the machines beeping and living for him that broke me though, and a sob escaped my throat before the tears returned with a flood's force.

"What happened?" Tesha asked.

"Things went sideways, and he saved my life. That caused him to get hit with two shots to his side, and there was internal damage. The third bullet hit him in the head, but it merely grazed him, so the doctors have assured me that he will make a full recovery," Umar replied.

"Who did this?" I asked, locking eyes with Umar.

I could tell right away that he didn't want to say anything, but he knew that silence wasn't an option.

"The less you know, the better," he replied.

"My daughter asked you a question, and as David's wife, she deserves an answer," Mom said, putting her hands on my shoulders.

"I understand that, but I also know that David would want her to stay away from all of this ugliness."

"It's too late for that. We're in it. Now tell us who the fuck did this so we know who to kill next," Tesha demanded in a menacing tone.

I could tell by the expression on Umar's face that he wasn't used to any woman speaking to him like this, but what he didn't understand was that none of us were going to get nicer about wanting answers. I stepped forward and took his hand in mine while looking up at him.

"Umar, when you married David and I, I told you that there was nothing I wouldn't do for him and with him. I meant that then, and I mean that even more now. Who did this to my husband?"

"A man by the name of Viktor Bah is responsible," he replied finally.

"Where is he?" Tesha asked.

"I don't know, but David managed to get off a couple shots, so I know Bah is injured. My men have his wife and daughter, but I haven't had a chance to question them my way yet."

"David is my husband, my world, and everything in it. I'll get the answers from them bitches. I guarantee you that."

Chapter 14

(David)
(Four Days Later)

When my eyes opened, I felt like I'd been asleep for a week straight. On the one hand, I felt rested, despite the aches in my body that reminded me immediately that I'd been shot. On the other hand, I felt disoriented as shit, like my thoughts were thick mud that I was trying to drag some heavy boots through. The fact that Tonya was the first person I saw didn't help my disoriented feeling because if anyone was to be sitting by my hospital bed, it would be my wife.

"Wh-Where's Ty?" I asked, clearing my throat in hopes of adding strength to my voice.

The pain that I felt rattle my insides with the vibration of my voice made me wince, but I embraced it. Pain meant life, and that was better than the death I felt lurking over me when I'd gotten shot.

"She'll be here in a little while. How are you feeling?" she asked, moving to the edge of her seat and taking my left hand in hers.

"Blessed."

"I know that's right. We're glad that you made it, and I talked to your doctor myself so that he could tell me that you'd make a full recovery," she said, smiling at me.

"My uncle... Is my uncle..."

"He's fine. Don't worry. He's been here every day, right along with me, Tesha, and Ty," she replied.

"Wh-What about Shaomi?"

"We didn't wanna upset her because she has to look after Dayjah, so we didn't say anything about what happened to you," she said.

I nodded in understanding, glad that my daughter hadn't been traumatized anymore by the bullshit attached to my life. I wanted nothing more than for my kids to be happy, healthy, and free to live their life without fear of their parents' sins. None of those things was guaranteed, no matter what I did, but it was still a goal.

"How are Tesha and Ty? The babies?" I asked, looking her in the eyes.

"As far as I know, everything is going fine and according to schedule. Of course both of them are stressed the fuck out, but I stay on their ass about eating and resting enough."

"Th-Thank you, Tonya. For real," I said, wanting to say more but knowing that it wasn't necessary.

"I would say that you're welcome, only I'm not sure that I deserve your thanks because I've made your life more complicated."

"How so?" I asked curiously.

I could tell that she was choosing her next words carefully, but before she spoke, she got up and closed the hospital room door and came back.

"David, I can't tell you all the emotions that I felt when we found out that you'd been shot. It was difficult to act like I was only concerned for my daughter's sake when the truth is that I've got feelings for you too. You're wise beyond your years, and you're just a different type of nigga than the average. I know that you think us having sex was just about me wanting the dick, and it was at first, but it's deeper than that now," she said, sitting on the edge of the bed beside me.

I didn't know what to say to her declarations because they were so unexpected, and I didn't know the intention she had for telling me this. The threat of death did different things to different people, and me being shot had obviously made Tonya more sentimental. It made me smile, and when I did, she let the radiance of her beauty shine through by returning my smile. It took me a second to realize that the pressure I felt under my hospital gown was real and not a side effect of my pain medication. After that, it only took seconds to realize that the pressure was her hand on my dick.

"Uh, T-Tonya, wait a minute..."

"Just relax, David. We're alone, and you know that I can keep a secret like a Swiss banker. Besides, you should enjoy being alive," she said, pushing my hospital gown up.

With the speed of a snake striking, she dipped her head and took my rapidly rising dick in between her soft lips. I felt the air rush from my lungs like an active volcano venting through the earth, accompanied by a moan that was foreign to my own ears. The heat of her, coupled with the wetness only found within the earth's core, gave the same feelings of being buried inside her pussy. My mind flashed back, and that only made my dick harder. The one and only time that we'd fucked, she'd taken dick like a champ, and the way she was bobbing slowly all the way up and back down with her head told me that this experience would be no different.

Even with my dick on full tilt, she was eating my inches with ease and perfection, making it hard to keep my back on the hospital bed. The pain of my gunshots was momentarily forgotten, and all I cared about was the magic show of hide and seek she was playing.

"T-Tonya!" I gasped, trying to warn her.

She popped my dick out of her mouth long enough to let her spit drizzle from her bottom lip down over the throbbing head of it, and then, she used her hand to slowly jack me off. Her mouth went to work on my balls, and she sucked them in between her lips like her favorite pieces of chocolate. Within seconds, I saw stars clouding my vision, and my hands flew into her long hair by themselves. My fingers locked themselves within her tresses like handcuffs, and I knew that in this moment, I was her prisoner. I could feel my climax coming fast, but all I could do was grunt unintelligibly. Suddenly, her mouth was back to work sucking my dick, only now she was increasing her speed with every nosedive into my pubic hair. My cum rocketed to the back of her throat with the force of a tractor trailer crashing into a car, and it felt so good that I almost passed out. She paused in her bobbing to drink all of my protein like it was her favorite shake and only when the last drop was absorbed did she lift her head all the way. The smile that she gave me transformed her beauty to gorgeousness, making it hard to believe that she'd done something so wonderfully nasty to me.

"Just the right amount of salt," she said, pulling my gown back down and returning to her seat beside my bed.

I was lost for words and not simply because she'd sucked coherent thought out of me. What the fuck did one say to the mother-in-law who sucked dick like a porn star on steroids? All I could do was lay there with a silly smile on my face.

"You good?" she asked.

"Mmm hmm."

"I'm glad because I've got something important to tell you," she said, turning suddenly serious.

Despite my mind still being way up with the clouds, I turned my head in her direction so that she would know I was listening.

"There's really no easy way to say this, David, and there will never be a right time, so... yeah, I'm pregnant with your baby," she said calmly.

It seemed like some type of audio delay between my brain and her words because what she'd said didn't register for a full thirty seconds. Then, I spent another thirty seconds trying to convince myself that she HADN'T said that she was carrying my child too, but then, my mind went back to the discussion we'd all had about family. Tonya had put both Tesha's and Tynesha's hands on her stomach and said the word family, but with everything going on, I'd forgotten to ask her about what she'd implied. I didn't have to ask her anymore nor did I have to question if she was serious because this stopped being a game long ago.

"Who knows?" I asked.

"Tesha and Ty but Ty doesn't know it's yours."

"But Tesha does of course," I said, understanding that Tesha and Tonya were carrying each other's dangerous secrets.

"You already know that Tesha isn't gonna say anything, but I'm more interested in what you have to say."

"What do you mean?" I asked slowly.

"I mean, are you gonna ask me to get an abortion?"

I couldn't tell what type of answer she wanted or expected, but all I could give her was honesty.

"That's not my call to make because it's your body, and I would never think to try and control it," I replied.

"I know that, David, but what do you want me to do? Do you want me to have the baby or not?"

I knew that the easy answer was no, but that decision would get harder to reconcile with my conscience as I got older and wiser. Of that, I was absolutely sure. I also knew that this was something that we both had to deal with, and it should be that way because we'd both made the reckless decision to fuck.

"I want all of my children because none of them were mistakes. They're blessings," I replied sincerely.

Her eyes quickly filled with tears as she nodded in agreement, but the sound of the door opening behind her kept them from falling.

"My nephew, you are awake," Umar said, quickly crossing the room to my bed's side.

Tonya took that moment to silently slide out of the room, probably going to compose herself, blowing me a kiss on the way out.

"I'm good, Uncle. How are you?"

"Now that you're awake, I can breathe again. It's been a long four days waiting on you to wake up."

"Four days?" I asked, surprised by how much time had passed.

"Yes, four whole days but the doctors here continued to reassure us that you would awaken and come back to us. I'm pleased that they were right, and I know that your wife will be just as excited."

"Speaking of which, where is Ty?" I asked.

The look on his face transformed so fast that it was almost hard to fathom, but the hard lines around his mouth weren't figments of the imagination.

"Uncle, what is it? Where is my wife?" I asked, feeling slight panic in my chest.

"She is physically okay so please don't worry yourself. Mentally and emotionally, it has been a very trying time for her and her sister."

"Well, that's understandable, but why do I feel like there's something you're not telling me?" I asked cautiously.

For a second, he just stared at me, weighing something that I couldn't see within the spaces of his mind. In the end, he chose to respond, not with words but by pulling his phone out and scrolling through it. I was on the verge of feeling ignored when he passed the phone to me, and I came face-to-face with two women strapped to chairs. It was hard to tell if they'd once been beautiful because their faces were disfigured by cuts, bruises, broken noses, fractured orbital bones, and a missing ear apiece.

"Who are they?" I asked.

"The daughter and wife of Councilman Bah."

"Who did this to them?" I asked, looking my uncle in the eyes.

"Your wife and her sister. Since you got shot, they've become... different. They move with only one goal, and that's to inflict maximum pain."

"Where are they now? I need to see them before they do something they can't come back from," I said, struggling to sit up.

"They're still at this location with these women."

"Take me to them. I need to see them, Uncle Umar. Please."

Chapter 15

(Tynesha)

"P-Please! I told you everything I k-know about my husband. I don't know where he is, but it's him that you want to kill, not me and my daughter!"

Even though I understood every word she'd said through her accent and broken jaw, none of it made a difference to me. All I knew was that my husband's pain had to be atoned for, and I didn't feel like we were there yet. For that reason, I went back to the exact spot I intended to hit on her foot, and then, I raised the sledgehammer high before swinging with major league force. The sound of her bones breaking made me feel a little better, but she didn't scream like her daughter had when I'd shattered both of her feet and ankles. This one passed straight the fuck out.

"Look, she shitted on herself, and it's runny," Tesha said, pointing and chuckling at the brown mess running down the back of the chair and onto the floor.

"I guess she had to go," I replied unflinchingly.

"Well, both of these bitches are unconscious now, so what do you wanna do, sis?"

The simple answer was that I really wanted to kill them, but Umar had explained that we needed them alive to lure Viktor's bitch ass out of hiding. My patience was wearing thin though with every moment that passed, and it was getting harder for me not to send these bitches into the afterlife. My conscience was clear on doing it too because the nigga that they loved had come for me and mine. We had to make everyone understand what the fuck family meant at the end of the day.

"We can take a break and go check on David. Umar's men will continue to guard the shipping container out here, plus these bitches couldn't run if they wanted to," I said, dropping the hammer on the ground and wiping the sweat off of my face.

"I don't know about you, bitch, but me and my baby are hungry, so we need to get some food on the way to the hospital."

"Your fat ass would be thinking about food at a time like this," I replied, shaking my head as I led us out into the humid midmorning air.

I could feel my shirt sticking to my body, drenched with sweat, and it made me feel nasty, but a shower now was pointless. Out here in the Glades, the temperature stayed right around 104° until the sun set, and then, it dropped down to about 90°. If the heat didn't kill you then the alligators damn sure would. It was an ideal location for games of torture, but this environment was an absolute hell nah for a pregnant woman. For a second, my child's welfare crossed my mind, but I quickly shuffled that thought to the back of my brain because I couldn't let being pregnant slow me down. I would move carefully and strategically, but I would move nonetheless. The sound of a vehicle approaching grabbed my attention and had me reaching for my pistol until I saw that it was Umar's SUV.

"You're a little jumpy, sis," Tesha teased, laughing.

"Remember that when the shooting starts, hoe."

We both stood by the Hellcat and waited on the Lincoln Navigator to pull up beside us. I expected to see Umar's face when the SUV came to a stop and the window slid down, but I got the shock of my life because it was my beautiful husband's face.

"Oh, my God, David!" I squealed, quickly pulling the door open and flinging myself into his arms.

"Be gentle with me, baby," he said, chuckling.

"Oh, I'm sorry, baby. I'm just so happy to see you!"

"I'm happy to see you too... but I expected to open my eyes and see you beside my hospital bed," he replied softly.

I pulled back slowly and looked up into his eyes, feeling slightly sheepish and knowing how my husband would react to what I'd done.

"I'm sorry, David. Truly. I just got caught up out here handling business, but we were just about to head to the hospital. Right, Tesha?"

"After we got something to eat but yeah," she replied from behind me.

"Let me out so that we can talk about the business you're handling," David insisted.

I hopped back out of the SUV and helped him down along with Tesha, who'd taken his other arm. I could see that he was trying hard not to wince, but he was definitely still in pain, which meant that his ass probably should've still been in the hospital.

"Baby, I would've come to you if you would've called, and you know that. There was no reason for you to leave the hospital and come way out here."

"I could argue that there's no reason for either of your pregnant asses to be out here," he replied, looking at Tesha and then me.

Me and my twin had discussed what David's reaction would be, so we were ready for this fight.

"Baby, why do you keep acting like being pregnant is some type of disability or something? Thinking that a pregnant woman has to sit around with her feet up, or be on her feet in the kitchen, is old and archaic as fuck. We're just as capable now as we were before we got pregnant, and I need you to treat us like it," I said sincerely.

"You know that she's right, David," Tesha chimed in.

"Okay, but before either of you were pregnant, you still weren't getting blood on your hands. That was my job," he replied.

"Just because you pulled the trigger doesn't mean that blood ain't on our hands too and shit don't stop just because you got shot, bae. Our lives are still in danger, and the opps ain't bout to wait on you to heal up so that it's a fair fight," I stated factually.

"And we all agreed to live and die by the definition of family, David. For all mine, I'll lay yours, remember?" Tesha asked.

"I remember," he replied, shaking his head with a look of begrudging annoyance on his face.

"Would you feel better if you knew with probable certainty that we could handle this?" I asked.

"That depends on what you mean by probable certainty," he said neutrally.

"Fair enough. T, help him get in the car while I talk to Umar real quick," I said, stepping back over to the SUV.

"Is everything okay, Tynesha?" Umar asked.

"Yeah, we're good, Uncle. Our guests are in there taking a nap, and they haven't provided any new information since my last update to you."

"I've got my people looking into the possible locations that his wife offered up, but I haven't heard anything back yet," he said.

"Well, you know that David isn't physically ready to handle the threat right now, so I'mma get him back to the house after a detour to let him see my team. Call me when you're ready for us to make our move."

"I will. As for the councilman's wife and daughter, I'm hearing that Viktor doesn't care enough about either of them to risk coming out of hiding. It could be a bluff, but I don't know," he said.

"Let's call his bluff."

Umar quietly contemplated what I said, and undoubtedly, he was thinking about the consequences behind choosing this path of more violence. His dark brown eyes told horror stories of the things he'd seen and done, but he kept those memories his ordinary. It wasn't obvious to me until he'd lost his wife, but David being shot had made it more pronounced. The windows to this man's soul showed darkness, utter and complete darkness, but I wasn't frightened by it in the slightest.

"I will do as you suggest, but I will do it my way. You tend to your husband, and I'll be in touch soon."

"Okay, Uncle," I said, turning and heading to the driver's side of the Hellcat.

"We good?" Tesha asked.

"Yeah, let's go to the hotel and then back home," I replied, hopping in and starting the car.

I made sure to drive carefully so that the ride was as smooth as possible for my husband's sake, and it took us about an hour to get to the Hyatt hotel in downtown Miami. We made our way to the fifth floor and knocked like we were expected. Before David could ask anything, the door was opened, and he saw a familiar face.

"Carrie, what are you doing here?" he asked, glancing at me.

"I'm working. What else? Plus, you can't seem to keep your ass out of trouble. Are you even supposed to be out of the hospital?"

"Don't start that fight. PLEASE," Tesha said, pushing past Carrie into the room.

David and I followed, and I led him to the bed where he could relax and rest. When the bathroom door opened behind me and David started to chuckle, I knew he'd seen a blast from the past.

"Don't be looking at me like I didn't wash my hands, nigga, because you know better. Make me smack the shit out of you already," Nyaisha threatened, smiling.

"You actually managed to get Nyaisha out of New York and come this far south? After she SWORE never to come down here again?" he asked, clearly impressed.

"It only took one phone call," I replied, smiling.

"Davie boy, stop playing like you ain't know I was a real bitch, been a real bitch and bout that action because I been putting in work when it comes to family. I'm from Queens, New York, my nigga, and we built different up there. Remember that," Nyaisha said.

The smile on my nigga's face let me know that I had his approval, and that made me feel good inside. My cousin, Nyaisha, aka New York Ny, was hands down one of my favorite people, and she always had been. Back in the day, she'd got in trouble in New York for cutting a bitch's face, so she'd had to spend a couple summers down here as her penance. Her being five years older than us let her take Florida by storm, and some people really referred to her as Hurricane Ny. Me and Tesha had just been along for the ride.

I'd always been confident in my looks, but Nyaisha showed me what being a bad bitch was all about. She stood at 5'4", weighing a cute one hundred thirty-five pounds, but the weight was all ass. She had nice titties, a flat stomach, and an ass that fit the description of a perfect Georgia peach. You would think that with a body like that, the bitch could at least have the decency to be plain in the face, or even ugly, but nope, not this bitch. She was gorgeous, rocking a diamond stud in her nose and lip gloss that was always popping. Her swag was different, but it was the unwavering confidence that had set her apart from other females in my mind. I'd learned that from her, and that was why I never took my looks too seriously because I was way more than beauty beneath the surface. The fact that most people got stuck on our looks made us more than dangerous. It made us lethal.

"What's the status, Carrie?" I asked.

"Okay, so, the councilman does have responsibilities that he can't avoid, which means he's gonna have to work from somewhere. I say we bomb his office and his home simultaneously."

"Would he be back to work so soon after getting shot?" Tesha asked.

"That depends on how bad he got hit," Nyaisha replied.

"We don't know the answer to that question because all David's uncle could tell us was that David got a few shots off," I said.

"I got two shots off, and they hit him in either his stomach or his lower body," David explained.

"That means that son could be bleeding out from a gut shot or trying to sew his dick back together," Nyaisha said, laughing.

"Exactly, but there's no way to know. We need to do more surveillance, and I can call in a favor to get a couple drones to make that part easier," Carrie offered.

"That sounds like a plan. You and Nyaisha stay down here to handle that while Tesha and I take David home, and then, we'll get ready to make our next move," I said.

"And what's your best move?" David asked, looking directly at me.

My response was to flash him a sexy smile and a wink before turning my attention on my sister.

"Tesha, I need you to call your lawyer and confirm the terms of your surrender so that we can get that problem from over our head. Ma will go to the courthouse with you so that you can bond out immediately."

"Wait, what?" David asked suddenly.

I halfway expected him to have questions, and Tesha and I had discussed this too, but the look on her face was different now. It was almost like if David didn't approve then she wasn't about to go through with the plans.

"David, we can't keep fighting multiple enemies at the same time because it's splitting our focus and limiting our moves, so we need to solve any problems that we can," I replied reasonably.

"I get what you're saying, but Tesha being locked up just creates a new problem for us to fix," he retorted.

"That won't be an issue because we already bought the judge," Carrie said, smiling mischievously.

I laughed because I saw the remainder of the argument die on my husband's tongue, and it was cute to see him speechless.

"We got this shit, Davie boy. Just sit back and take notes, nigga," Nyaisha instructed, running her fingers through her braids.

"Yeah, I hear," he replied skeptically.

"My dear, sweet husband, I think it's time that you realize that the power of pussy is about more than the pressure it puts on men's souls. We run the world with this shit so learn to follow my lead."

Chapter 16

(David)
(One Week Later)

"Daddy, I made you a picture," Dayjah announced, coming into the living room with a piece of paper in hand.

"Let me see, sweetheart."

"It's me, you, and Mommy," she said with a huge grin.

"This is perfect, baby. Did you show your mommy?"

The fast movement of her head shaking sent her beads flying and banging together, which caused her to giggle with delight.

"Go show Mommy," I instructed, passing her the picture back.

Immediately, she took off like there were jet packs in her shoes, and I could swear that her feet were barely on the ground. Her pure, little kid joy always put a smile on my face, and today was no different.

"What are you grinning about?" Tonya asked, coming toward me with a plate of food in hand.

"Dayjah and all her innocence."

"That daughter of yours is a trip, but she's so happy that it's hard for anyone else not to be when you're around her. Have you thought about what you're gonna do if you end up with all girls?" Tonya asked, sitting down beside me on the couch.

I took the plate from her hands when she offered it to me and inhaled the rich aromas of fried chicken, macaroni and cheese, and sweet potatoes. Since I'd been on the injury reserve list, Tonya had added at least ten pounds to me with all the cooking that she'd done. At first, I tried to tell her that it was unnecessary for her to do all of that, but I quickly became spoiled by it and ceased putting up any kind of fight.

Somehow food was the one thing that brought all of my children's mothers together because I'd hear them in the kitchen laughing and joking while working in harmony. I was surprised and leery when Shaomi got involved, but I'd quickly learned that this bonding experience went back to their childhood. It actually seemed to smooth shit out between Shaomi and Ty, which definitely made my life easier. When we'd first got back from Miami, everybody had gotten cussed the fuck out by Shaomi for keeping her in the dark about me being shot, and I didn't fault her for being angry. Now that that storm had passed, everyone was getting along, and that was helping me heal quicker.

"God has a sense of humor, Tonya, but not even he's that damn funny to give me all girls," I said.

She leaned in close and put her lips to my ear.

"I don't know, but this pregnancy feels like it did when I had Tesha and Tynesha."

I almost choked on my food at the idea of having twins, which made Tonga's petty ass cackle with laughter.

"Ma, I told you not to try and kill my husband. Besides, I ain't got that new life insurance policy yet," Ty said, walking in and swiping a piece of chicken off of my plate as she sat on the other side of me.

"I wasn't trying to kill him, baby. I was just reminding him that twins run in the family."

This statement stopped the chicken in mid-flight to Ty's mouth, and the look on her face became one of sheer terror. That only made Tonya laugh harder as she got up and headed back toward the kitchen.

"Twins," Ty croaked, shaking her head slowly.

We looked at each other, and I could tell that we were thinking along the same lines of not being ready for twins. At this point, there was nothing that we could do besides wait and see. The sound of the front door opening and closing diverted our attention from the fear building in our minds.

"I could smell the chicken as soon as I got off of the elevator, so where is it?" Tesha asked, licking her lips.

"In the kitchen with your hungry ass," Ty replied.

"Says the big girl with a piece of chicken in her grip," Tesha said, laughing and heading straight toward the kitchen.

Ty laughed too, but I noticed that she didn't let that piece of chicken go.

"Baby, it's okay. I don't mind you feeding you and our child, but you better not think it's cute to steal food off of a big nigga's plate again," I said, leaning in and kissing her quickly on the lips.

Her smile was radiant, and it warmed my heart while also making me consider putting down my plate so that I could talk to her in our bedroom for a few minutes.

"You know that I'm healed from my injuries, right?" I asked innocently.

She laughed loudly, and I could see that she had a clear understanding along with that twinkle of mischief in her eyes. She even managed to bite the chicken in a seductive way.

"David, I need to talk to you," Shaomi said.

When I looked over and saw her standing just inside the living room, the smile that I'd felt on my face slipped away. Shaomi didn't look angry; she looked dead serious, and that meant that the topic of whatever conversation she wanted to have was important. I glanced at Ty to kind of check her temperature, but she was pretending to be completely captivated by the chicken in her mouth. When I passed her my plate of food though, she readily accepted it, which made me chuckle as I stood up and went to see what Shaomi wanted. I'd expected her to lead me back to her bedroom, but instead, she took me out to the balcony, and my mind immediately flashed back to the last time we'd been here.

"What's up, Sha Sha?"

"I didn't wanna say anything while you were healing up, but now that you're more or less back to normal, we need to discuss Dayjah."

"Okay. What about Dayjah?" I asked.

"When you took me to Georgia to get her, we both agreed to send her to Ghana with your family where she'd be safe, and I need you to honor that promise."

"Do you think that we can't protect her here anymore or something?" I asked, wondering where this was coming from.

"I'm not saying that. I'm simply reminding you of what the plan was that we agreed to before we took her out of the safe place that she was in."

"You're right. That's what we agreed to, but... I'm bonding with her, and she's finally used to being around her parents," I explained.

"I get that. I really do, and I don't want to send her away, but I don't wanna lose her or for her to see one of us die. I don't want to cause her any more trauma than she's already been subjected to, and neither of us can guarantee that it won't happen if she stays. Every moment that I've ever spent away from her has torn me up inside but doing what's best for her comes before my feelings. As much as I know it's gonna hurt you, David, I need you to put her needs in front of your feelings."

Even though her words were spoken with care and love, they still hit hard like Grandma's backhand from childhood. I loved my daughter and all my unborn children with all of my heart and soul, so I'd do anything for them. No matter how badly it hurt me, I pulled my phone from my pocket and dialed my Uncle Umar's number before putting the phone on speaker to allow Shaomi to hear.

"Hello, my nephew. How are you holding up?"

"I'm good, Uncle. Almost completely healed and ready to get back to the fight. That brings me to my reason for calling because Shaomi and I agree that it's time to send Dayjah some place safe, and Ghana is the safest place that I know."

"I understand. I understand. When would you like to send her?" he asked.

"Actually, I think it would be better if we took her there ourselves," Shaomi blurted out.

The surprise that I felt was genuine, but the idea took root in my mind quickly, and I liked it because it gave us a chance to put Dayjah at ease.

"Do you both have valid passports?" he asked.

When I looked at Shaomi, she nodded that she did.

"Yes, Uncle, we do."

"Okay then. I will book us a flight right away and call you back with the details," he replied.

"Thank you," Shaomi said.

"No need to thank me. It's what family does for one another," he stated before disconnecting the call.

"It'll make it easier for her with us both being there, so that was a good call on your behalf," I said.

"So, you're not mad? I wasn't trying to be rude by jumping into your conversation, but..."

"Nah, you're good. I get it. I just don't know how I'm gonna explain this to Tynesha," I mumbled.

The look on her face was something between amusement and sympathy, and it was cute even though it didn't help me a damn bit. I took a breath before turning and going back inside to my spot on the couch. I was more than a little surprised to find the same amount of food on my plate as when I'd handed it to Ty when she handed it back to me.

"You could've eaten, bae."

"For some reason, I lost my appetite," she replied dryly.

I didn't even have to look at her to know that her appetite and attitude were directly tied to Shaomi pulling up on me. Putting the plate on the coffee table allowed me to pull her into my arms and holding her was the only thing I did for five minutes. I just held her and listened to her breathe.

"Is what you're about to tell me that bad that you needed to make sure I felt physically safe and emotionally secure?" she asked, looking up at me.

"It's not that it's necessarily bad. I just know that you're not gonna like it."

"Okay, well, spit it out because the anxiety alone makes me wanna go a few rounds with her," she said sincerely.

"Don't do that, sweetheart. She just came to remind me of my promise to keep Dayjah safe by sending her to Ghana, and she thinks it's time to make that happen."

"Okay... and what do you think?" she asked, still looking at me.

"I mean, to be real with you, baby, I wanted to keep my daughter here because I've missed so much time with her already. I don't want her to continue to be affected by the war we're caught in the middle of though, and I definitely don't want her to see any of us die. So, I agreed with Shaomi about moving her out of the country."

I got the nod of understanding from the woman in my arms, but that still wasn't enough to relax me just yet because there was an expectant look in her eyes.

"Why are you looking at me like that?" I asked.

"Because I'm waiting on you to finish. I know based on your delicate approach that there has to be more to the story."

I hesitated, not out of fear of my wife's reaction but just because I had to ask myself if there could possibly be an ulterior motive on Shaomi's part.

"You're right. There's more. I told Uncle Umar that Shaomi and I would bring Dayjah to Ghana ourselves in hopes of making the separation easier all the way around the board," I replied.

"Of course you did, baby, because you're gonna miss her and because it's gonna be an adjustment for her. It'll be nice to get away with you for a few days though, and this will be our first trip out of the country together."

Her words sounded the alarm in my brain, and I knew shit was going bad at the next turn.

"Baby, you never been out of the country, right?" I asked.

"Nope, and that's why I'm low key excited!"

"Okay, so I need you to slow down and listen to me for a second. I would LOVE to show you the Motherland, especially because we get the royal treatment over there, but there are two issues. The first is that you haven't been vaccinated, and that's a mandatory with you being pregnant going into a foreign country. The second problem is that you don't have a passport, and you need that to do any type of international travelling," I said gently.

Her mouth opened quickly to say something, and I braced for the explosion, but not a word or sound came out. The hazel green in her eyes flashed like a beautiful summer lightning storm, but I resisted the urge to flirt.

"So, you're saying that it's just you, Shaomi, and Dayjah going then," she finally said.

"Baby, I'll be back in a few days. It's not a vacation. We're just dropping off our daughter and..."

"I get it, David. I get it. I'm not mad. I just want you to be safe out there," she said, moving out of my arms and standing up.

Before I could speak again, she was moving away from me.

"Ty, where are you going?"

"To say goodbye to Dayjah. I want her to know that she'll be loved and missed because, in case you forgot, my husband, she's supposed to be my daughter too."

Chapter 17

(Tynesha)
(Two Days Later)

In my lifetime, I'd noticed that the moments of my most profound reflection came during the times I was the most stressed. This time was no different. Here it was 3 a.m., and while I should've been asleep and dreaming, I was instead staring at the ceiling while the coldness of the spot in the bed next to me seemed to laugh. If David had been here, I could've used sex or conversation as a distraction from my insomnia, but then again, if he had been here then I might not have a reason to reflect. I was only days away from my twenty-second birthday, and even though I was married with a child on the way, I still didn't feel like I'd accomplished what I'd wished for at this time last year. Granted, I was happier than I'd ever been now that Roland was out of my life, but I still didn't have what anyone would call a normal relationship. David was good to me, and I knew that he loved me, but if I was honest then I knew that normal might never describe what we were. I was different with him and because of him, which wasn't necessarily a bad thing. It just wasn't what I envisioned it would be. The love was real though, and that was what I was clinging to with all my heart and soul. I'd never loved or been loved like I was when I was with David, and I knew just how rare what we had was. For that reason alone, I'd ride and die with my nigga.

I just wished there weren't certain complications and by that I meant my husband having a baby by my cousin. Yeah, it was before him and I, and yeah, we could all coexist, but that shit made me feel some type of way. Maybe it was the fact that I couldn't get past it that made me feel some type of way but part of me felt like that would be any bitch's normal response. It wasn't like he cheated on me or still had feelings for her, which made me believe that it was just my intuition picking up on her feelings for him. The uncertainty of questions and answers continued to plague me until the sun finally came up outside my window, coaxing me out of bed with it. I smoked a blunt to combat the morning sickness that still popped up occasionally, and then, I went to the kitchen in search of food.

"You're up early," Tesha said from her seat at the kitchen table.

"Ditto, bitch."

"Yeah, well, you can blame your niece or nephew for that shit," she replied, putting a hand on her stomach.

I could see the love for her child on her face, and for a second, I wondered what kind of mothers we would be. Would we smother our kids and isolate them from the big, bad world? Or would we guide them as our mother had done to ensure that they not only survived but thrived within that big, bad world? Only time would tell.

"Are you okay?"

"Oh, yeah, I'm great, but the morning sickness ain't no bitch sometimes, even with the weed to help," she replied.

"Don't I know it. Are you hungry because I can whip us up something real quick?"

"Bitch, you know that I'm hungry because we're on the same feeding schedule! Before we get to that though, why don't you come over here and tell me what's bothering you?" she said, pulling a chair out for me.

I felt suddenly self-conscious about speaking my thoughts aloud that had kept me up all night, but I pushed those feelings away with the understanding that me and my twin didn't have secrets for real. I grabbed the box of donuts from off the top of the refrigerator and sat down at the table next to her.

"Pass me one with sprinkles," she demanded immediately.

"Fat ass," I said under my breath, chuckling.

"Like you got room to talk, hoe! Do you wanna talk about what happened to the leftover chicken? That was mass murder if I've ever seen it, and you ain't leave a witness to the crime with your hungry ass!"

"You got that one. You got that one," I replied, laughing and passing her the donut she wanted.

Once I'd bitten into my own chocolate éclair, I was ready for some girl talk.

"Okay, so, I'm probably tripping, and I can own that part, but the fact that Shaomi has a whole kid with my nigga is still fucking with me," I confessed.

"You too?"

"Wait, so I'm not tripping?" I quickly asked.

"I mean, yes and no. I'mma say no because it's hella weird that our cousin has a baby with him AND she lied about it, but I say yes because there's nothing you can do about it. Whether we like it or not, her and David are tied together for life."

"Unless that's not really his baby," I blurted.

"Say what?! Biiittttcccccchhhh! Is this tea that you're spilling or wishful thinking?" she asked eagerly, turning her chair to face me.

"Wishful thinking but I mean, shit, if the bitch will tell the one lie then we know what she's capable of. I've had my eye on her because something in my gut tells me she wants more than a co-parenting relationship with David. I think Shaomi wants..."

"Him," Tesha stated, nodding her head in agreement.

"Bitch, is this tea that YOU'RE spilling?" I asked, looking at her closely.

"Nah, no tea and nothing factual to stand on. I just get the same intuitive feelings that you get, which brings me to my next question. How the fuck did you let that nigga convince you to let him go with Shaomi and Dayjah to Africa without your silly ass?!"

"I don't have a passport, and I haven't been vaccinated," I replied lamely.

"And Mommy said that you can't go outside until all your homework is done! Bitch, I know that you didn't let that sucka shit keep you locked in this fucking castle like Princess Fiona!"

Her words had the instant effect of making me feel foolish, and I was questioning myself now more than ever.

"What was I supposed to do, Tesha? The nigga all but told me to sit my ass down and play my position."

"Right, and your position is that nigga wife! Let me ask you this, Ty, and be real with me. Do you think Shaomi wants David back?"

"I mean, yeah, but it's just a feeling."

"No, sis. It's a gut feeling, and that shit hits a little different. Now you already know that I slept in her room last night to be up here with you. What you didn't know is that when I got up and used the bathroom this morning, I found Shaomi's birth control. That left me with two questions; who is she fucking, and why didn't those pills catch a flight with her scandalous ass? I know that David loves you, and I'm not trying to make you doubt that, but he's a man, baby, and that means he's a slave to the pussy."

Suddenly, the taste of the donut on my tongue filled me with a nauseous feeling, but I managed not to throw up. What I couldn't manage were the million and one thoughts that had flooded my mind after diving off the deep end of her last two questions. No one could make me doubt David's love... but no one could make me deny my intimate knowledge of pussy power.

"What am I supposed to do?" I asked, feeling lost and pissed off at the same time.

"Do you wanna go to Africa?"

"I mean, yeah, but..."

"Shhh with the bullshit and trust your twin," she said, pulling her phone out with a huge grin on her face.

I waited curiously as she typed out a text with lightning speed and sent it flying through the clouds.

"Who are you texting at this time of the morning?" I asked.

"A friend and it's not early where he's at."

"Hold up, bitch. I know that ain't a smile I see on your face! Who is this nigga because friends don't make your pretty ass blush," I said, studying her closely.

Her laughter rang out with melodic tones that could only translate into excitement for anyone hearing it, and the flushed look on her face spoke of one word to me. Love.

"I mean, he is a friend, but you know how it goes."

"Nah, I don't know so fucking explain it to me and start from the beginning," I replied, laughing.

"Okay, soooo, his name is Royal Walker, and I met him a while ago on Instagram. He'd liked a few of my pix on Facebook before following me on the Gram, and one day, he slid into my messages. I checked his pix, and he was cute or whatever, so I decided to give him five minutes of my time."

"And that's all it took to have you with that goofy ass look on your face?" I asked, impressed.

"Sis, it's gonna sound corny, but the nigga is so different from others that I've known. He's eighteen, but he's got that old soul wisdom that only comes through experience. What made me give him the first five minutes was the fact that he didn't come with some lame lines just because I was cute. He wanted to know what was keeping my ears from touching."

At first, I looked at her, confused, but then, I understood that he WAS checking her mental.

"Okay, well, you ain't never been dumb, but can he keep up is the question?" I asked.

"Mmm hmm. He's in Nigeria right now, and he's already seen the world damn near twice, which has only enhanced his maturity. Don't get me wrong though because the nigga ain't perfect, and he comes with a past like we all do, but he was up front about that with me."

"What kind of past?" I asked suspiciously.

Her hesitation made my spider sense tingle because it was entirely possible for any female to be blind to red flags of a nigga if she wanted to be. I wasn't about to let no fast talking, pretty nigga play with my twin's heart though.

"Talk to me, Tesha. You know that I got you."

"I know you do, but... Okay, so when I say that he's got a past, I mean that his hands ain't exactly clean, and he comes from a family that's with the shit," she explained.

"Exactly how with the shit are they?"

"Well, if there was ever a family that defined 'for all mine, I'll lay yours,' it would be him and his people," she replied.

"Royal Walker? I don't remember the first name, but the last name does sound vaguely familiar now that you're saying all of this."

"Do you remember back when we were in high school, and there was this massive international manhunt for these three sisters? Freedom, Angel, and Destiny Walker?" she asked casually.

Instantly, my mind flashed back to breaking news headlines I had seen about buildings being bombed, people being savagely murdered, and the gorgeous women accused of it all. There was one other face that I saw too, and I remembered the sheer terror of him making my panties wet as a young girl.

"You're talking about the daughters of Jonathan 'FatherGod' Walker."

"Yeah, that's exactly who I'm talking about," she agreed.

"Okay... and?"

"Royal is FatherGod's son, and those are his sisters," she said nonchalantly.

"Ohhhh, shit," I replied, wide eyed.

"Ty, please don't judge him because..."

"I'm not. I promise. It was just a little bit of a shock, that's all, but it's cool. If you like it then I love it for you," I said sincerely.

"I do like him, but we're taking things slowly right now."

The sound of her phone pinging had her looking at her screen, and the smile that lit up her face looked like she was halfway in love with him already.

"Okay, so make it make sense for me and tell me what you texted him as far as it relates to this situation."

"Well, Royal and I have been wanting to see each other in person, and he's invited me to see Nigeria a bunch of times, so I figured we'd take him up on his offer. The plane will be here later today."

"The plane?" I asked.

"Yeah, he said that he'd send a private jet to get us because he wants us to fly comfortably with us being pregnant."

"Wait, you actually told him that you're pregnant with another nigga's baby?" I asked, surprised by this.

"Oh, yeah, he knows. We talk about everything. He's not scared of being around kids because he had to raise his little brother and cousin on his own for almost two years when he was really young. I think it was when his sisters were being hunted by every law enforcement agency on the damn planet."

"Okay but wait. We still don't have passports," I reminded her.

"Ty, will you stop worrying so much and just trust your twin? I got this, and all you gotta do is find out where David is staying without tipping your hand and telling him that we're about to pull the ultimate pop up on that ass!"

The thought of the expression on his face made me giggle as I pulled my sister into a hug as my way of thanking her.

"Are we telling Mom about this?" I asked.

"Why not? She always enjoys a well thought out plan. The first thing that we need to do though is schedule our hair and nail appointments. My first impression gotta be on point," she replied, pulling back and looking at my hair.

I self-consciously smoothed down my ponytail, but the idea of reminding David that he still had the baddest bitch in the game made me smile.

"Shit, I'm down with that, and I'mma hit Carrie and Nyaisha up so that they can come with us. Do you wanna have an early dinner at our favorite restaurant since we'll be out of town on our actual birthday?"

"You read my mind, bitch!" she exclaimed excitedly.

"Aight then. Let's get in motion, sis. We back outside!"

Chapter 18

(David)

"Daddy, look! Giraffes!" Dayjah squealed excitedly, jumping up and down while pointing at the majestic animals.

"I see them, baby. I see them. They're beautiful."

"Mom, come see the giraffes!" Dayjah yelled.

A few seconds later, Shaomi stepped out of the house onto the back veranda with us, carrying a strawberry daiquiri in her hand. Our eyes locked as she sauntered over to the railing where Dayjah stood looking down and out into the open desert, and I could tell that she was happy. Something about being here had relaxed Shaomi in a way that I'd never seen from her when we were back in the states, and it looked good on her. Even the sway of her hips was different, which was why my eyes were fixated on her bikini bottoms right now. I knew that this wasn't some exotic vacation for lovers, but it was hard to deny that Shaomi had been giving me that look since we'd gotten here. If what happened in Vegas stayed in Vegas, then I had to have a free pass by being in another country where I was royalty. At first, it was weird for Shaomi to see people treat me so different, but as the future king of the Asante tribe, I was given an extreme amount of respect. You could visit different parts of Africa and find all different types of government in positions of power, but tribal rule was still a sacred thing. The house we were staying in was a ten-bedroom mansion that was first built by my ancestors, and it had been preserved through the generations. My uncle stayed here when he was in town, but he also maintained a penthouse apartment in Johannesburg for whenever he had to go handle business. In following with tradition, our family's main business was import/export, but I had yet to familiarize myself with the ins and outs of it. Ever since we'd touched down, I'd wondered if Tynesha could see herself living here permanently because part of me was already adjusting to the idea. The feeling of freedom watching my daughter enjoy and experience her heritage was so peaceful that it was completely foreign to me but welcome nonetheless. Moving the whole family out here was something that I was envisioning, but there was still work to do before riding off into a gorgeous sunset could be entertained.

"What are you over here thinking about with that half a smirk on your face?" Shaomi asked, sitting down across from me in a lounge chair.

"The future. That's all."

"Oh, yeah? Am I somewhere in that vision?" she asked casually.

"How could you not be, Sha Sha? You're Dayjah's mom."

"I know that, David. She did come out of my pussy. That's not what I'm talking about though, and you know that, so let's have a real conversation."

"Okay. What do you wanna talk about?" I asked, mentally shifting my focus.

"I wanna talk about you, me, and the unfinished business of us. I understand that you're married to Tynesha, but are you gonna lie and say that you don't still have love for me?"

"I'll always have love for you," I admitted readily.

"But?"

"But if you're suggesting or asking me to leave my wife, then the answer is no," I replied honestly.

"I won't lie and act like I don't want you all to myself, David, but given the situation, I'm more than willing to compromise by sharing you. As long as we have an understanding."

I knew better than to play this game with her, but I could feel my curiosity already getting the best of me in the worst way.

"An understanding like what exactly?"

"I expect you to keep shit cute for the sake of everyone's feelings and not just your wife. I can respect her position and keep whatever happens between me and you, our business only. But I don't want you to carry me like some bum bitch because I ain't never been that. I'm not on birth control because I can't have any more kids, which means that all that can come from us fucking is shared pleasure. I don't want it to just be about sex though. You were my best friend, my Davie Crockett, and I missed that," she confessed, smiling.

I could feel the corners of my mouth tilting upwards in response to her, which prompted her to reach her hand across the glass table between us.

"Oh, you wanna shake on it?" I asked, chuckling.

"Absolutely. You're still a man of your word, right?"

I stared at her long and hard, assessing the mischief on display with the familiarity of someone seeing an old favorite movie. What she was suggesting sounded easy, but I was questioning whether or not either of us were being honest about the unpredictability of emotions. The last thing that I wanted to do was hurt Shaomi in any way, and the thought of that possibility turned my eyes toward our daughter a few feet away. Dayjah's happiness and security came first, and I knew that because she was still so young that her emotions were tightly tied to her parents. This decision made it easy to justify my decision.

"You got my word," I finally said, extending my hand across the table as I locked eyes with her.

"Thanks, bestie!"

"Shut up sounding like Barbie," I said, laughing.

Her tongue shot out of her mouth to go with the screw face she was giving me, but my phone started ringing before I could heat her ass up with jokes. Seeing that it was Ty calling made my heart beat faster with paranoia, but I ignored that and answered the Facetime call.

"What's up, baby? You good?" I asked, smiling into my phone's camera.

"Hey, husband! Yeah, I'm good, just out getting a manicure and pedicure with my girls."

The view suddenly changed, and I saw Tesha and Tonya waving at me before Ty spun the camera in the opposite direction, and I saw Nyaisha and Carrie.

"Okay, I see you all out there living your best lives and shit. Go ahead and charge it all to my account," I instructed.

"Awww, that's sweet of you, baby, but don't play like a bitch can't put a dent in your credit card."

"Do your worst and just consider it the warmup for your birthday," I replied.

"Well, thank you, my love, but you know that all I really want for my birthday is..."

"Easy, baby! Dayjah is within earshot," I warned, chuckling.

I could feel Shaomi's eyes on me from across the table, but I knew that now definitely wasn't the time to look up. Ty laughed out loud while shaking her head.

"See, your mind is already on getting some, but I wasn't even about to go there. I was just gonna say that all I want is you, so will you be back by then?" she asked, looking hopeful.

"Of course, bae. Dayjah is adjusting great to the family and the staff that works in the house, so we think she'll be ready to meet her cousins tomorrow."

"That's good, but did you say that you have a staff of people working in your house? How big is the damn house?" she asked.

"Technically, it's an estate, but I'll give you the tour real quick," I said, getting up and heading inside.

It was almost forty-five minutes later when I was done showing and explaining the history behind everything. The interest that Ty showed in everything gave me hope for the possibility that she would agree to relocate here permanently once we'd finished our business in Florida. After our call was over, I went in search of Shaomi and Dayjah, but I only found one of the two out by the infinity pool.

"Where's Dayjah?"

"One of your aunts took her to get a chocolate chip cookie before putting her to bed. She missed her nap today, so she was a little cranky, and I wanted her to be well rested in order to keep up with her cousins tomorrow."

"Makes sense. So, what are you about to get into?" I asked, looking around.

"Oh, well, I was just waiting on you to see if I could entice you into a night swim," she replied, standing up so that we were standing toe to toe.

I looked at her for a few moments, feeling something in the pit of my stomach that I couldn't put an exact description to.

"I'm down for a swim, just let me go get my trunks real quick."

"You don't have to do that on my account, baby. I mean, it's not like I haven't sewn you naked before," she said, smiling widely.

Before I could move or respond, she reached up and pulled the string to her bikini's top, allowing her titties to spill out into the moonlight. My eyes didn't move away from her face, which she must've taken as some type of challenge because the next thing I knew, she was untying the bikini bottoms too. She tossed both pieces of fabric to me as she turned and executed a dive of perfect form into the clear blue water. I watched her swim the length of the pool, admiring the grace and sexiness of her body while questioning the door that I'd opened with this game of cat and mouse.

I finally made the decision to turn my brain off and just go with the flow. I tossed her bikini on the lounge chair and quickly added all of my clothes to the pile before executing a perfect cannonball into the crisp water. When I broke the surface, she was right there in front of me, and I knew what was coming, so I took a big breath. Immediately, she started the water fight by pushing with all of her might in my direction, and I could hear the joy in her laughter. The wave she created hit me flush in the face, but I was already going back under water on the attack. Before she knew what hit her, I'd grabbed her by her hips, used the bottom of the pool as my springboard, and launched her backwards through the air. Her laughter quickly turned into playful screams, and the battle was on like the many summer days we'd spent back home at the public pool. For the first time since way back then, I felt like a carefree kid again, and I was loving every moment of it. After a while, we ended up in the shallow end of the pool, sitting on the steps, trying to catch our breath.

"That was fun," I said, smiling at her.

"Yeah, it was, but we ain't done yet."

She followed her words with actions by moving toward me and swiftly straddling me. Her mouth greeted mine with a hunger that was familiar and reciprocated in kind as my hands went to her braids. Within seconds, my dick was hard and demanding, but she was already answering the need by taking ahold of it and easing her hot pussy down on it. She was so tight that I was afraid to blink, lest my eye movement alone be too much motion and I cum quick. Being in the water forced us to move slowly, which made everything feel like a water ballet production. I could feel the tension rolling through her body, and for a second, I wondered if our kinetic energy could create electricity under water. Death would be as sweet as I knew her pussy tasted. Before we'd actually gotten to this point, I'd thought I was prepared to stand up inside her all night like I used to, but my climax was a demanding hunger that I couldn't ignore. The sudden ringing of my phone a few feet away made me pause but only for a split second because I just picked Shaomi up and carried her out of the pool with me. The moment that we were completely free of the water, I was able to push all of my dick up inside her, forcing my name to fall from her lips sensually. She felt so damn good that I pulled her off me, put her on her feet, and spun her around so that I could bend her little ass over. My left hand was already wrapping her braids around my fingers as I pushed my dick back inside her, and then, I was fucking her like making her head pop off into the pool was my goal. My phone was still ringing but only my death could get me out of this race to fulfilment. A few seconds later, her pussy grip went from handshake straight to a punishing vise grip that robbed me of my cum as she gushed on me. By the time I finished convulsing in passion, I could barely stand, which forced me to pull her into my arms and collapse with her on the closest lounge chair.

"You-you missed me too, huh?" She panted, laughing with satisfaction.

There was no denying the truth in her statement, at least from my body's standpoint, so I didn't even try. Instead, I grabbed my pants to see whose call I'd missed. There was no text message, just a voicemail that I accessed and put on speaker while laying back. The moment that I heard Ty's voice, my blood went cold, and her words made my heart stop altogether.

"David... Help."

Chapter 19

(Tynesha)

"Alright, so what's the move because you already know that a bitch gotta get dressed before we hit the town," Nyaisha said once we were all standing on the sidewalk out front of the nail shop.

"We all gotta get dressed, bitch. You ain't bout to upstage shit over here," Tesha said.

Nyaisha looked at all of us with a serious expression, and then, she laughed.

"It's all good because I only travel with a team of baddies, so are we headed back to your spot?" Nyaisha asked.

"Let's split up so that we can multitask. Me and Tesha will go make our reservations in person so that we can scoop up our outfits from the boutique. The rest of you can go back to our spot and get dressed. Ma, you got the key to the first-floor apartment," I said, nodding at her.

"That's what's up. We'll catch up with you in a minute," Nyaisha said.

Her, my mom, and Carrie got into Carrie's blue Ford Expedition while me and Tesha headed toward the Hellcat.

"I'mma get David to buy me a new car for my birthday," I said, thinking out loud.

"Don't forget that we're twins so I'mma need that same treatment, and I'll be sure to tell him that. By the way, I loved how you played that whole conversation with him to get him to expose his location," she said, smiling as she got in on the passenger side.

"You already know that I been the queen of finessing a nigga."

We both laughed at that as I hopped in, and we pulled off.

"Do you think the cake is ready?" she asked.

"I mean, it should be because that was the first call I made this morning once we decided to speed up our birthday plans."

"Cool, so we might as well pick that bad muthafucka up first since the bakery is on the way to the boutique," she suggested.

"Listen to you, bitch. You're damn near singing now that your fat ass is thinking about that strawberry Oreo cake!" I said, laughing.

"Whatever, hoe. That ain't even what's got a bitch ready to start an R&B career."

Her words caused me to look over at her, and the shit eating grin on her face said it all.

"Oh, this has nothing to do with cake and everything to do with your sweet tooth for a certain Royal treat," I teased.

"Shut up! You got a bitch over here blushing and shit!"

"That ain't me, sis. That's ALL ROYAL! I can't wait to meet the nigga that got you spun like this, and you ain't even smelled the dick yet. You probably couldn't pick that muthafucka out of a lineup!" I said, laughing loudly.

"You a muthafuckin lie, bitch, because I've seen that pretty ass dick he working with!"

Her declaration only made me laugh harder, and she couldn't help but to join in on the hysterics. The only thing that made our laughter subside was the sound of her phone going off with an incoming call. The speed of her reaction told me who the Usher ringtone of *Daddy's Home* belonged to, and that sent me into a laughing fit again.

"Bitch, will you shut up?!" she demanded, smoothing her hair down and checking her teeth.

All I could do was clap a hand over my mouth and let her be great.

"Hey, handsome. What's up?" she asked, smiling seductively.

I started to point this out too, but I didn't want to embarrass my twin.

"I'm good, beautiful, and we just leveled off at thirty thousand feet," he replied.

"Oh, my God, you're really on your way?" she asked, sounding so giddy that I had to look over at her again.

I saw her phone's screen move away from the fine ass, brown skin nigga with the easy smile to a stunning starry sky view and then back to him.

"I told you that I'd be there as soon as you were ready," he said smoothly.

"You're right. You did. I guess I'm just used to niggas selling dreams," she admitted.

"I'd rather dream with you before I'd ever sell you one, sweetheart," he replied quickly.

"Mmph!" I grunted approvingly.

His laugh was rhythmic to the point of being hypnotic, and it made her turn a bright shade of red before she spun the phone toward me.

"That's my sister with the sound effects," Tesha said.

"What's up?" he said.

"Hi, it's nice to finally put a face to the name," I said.

'Likewise," he replied.

"I just wanna thank you for coming out here to..."

In the blink of an eye, Tesha's phone went flying into the windshield as her body rocked hard enough to smack into me. The sounds of grinding metal and breaking glass were what triggered my brain into recognizing that we were in a car accident. I couldn't get control of the spinning steering wheel in front of me though, and that caused feelings of panic. I could feel the car sliding and spinning to my left, and then, my vision was filled with the sight of a looming utility pole rushing toward us. The impact knocked the wind out of me, and I felt myself sliding into unconsciousness as the car finally settled into its resting place. It took everything in me to fight back against the darkness pulling me under, but the unmistakable smell of gasoline was a hell of a motivator.

"T-Tesha? T, are you okay?" I asked weakly, looking over at her.

She was slumped toward me, making it impossible for me to see her face, but it was clear that she was unconscious.

"Tesha?" I called again, trying to take off my seatbelt.

Seeing her door mangled told me that she'd taken the brunt of the force, and it looked like she was pinned down. I struggled to get my phone out of my pocket, and then, I called David. As it rang, I took mental stock of myself, feeling the cut on my forehead that was bleeding and checking for more. My entire body hurt, and the fear that brought about the fate of my child made the panic take a firmer grip of my mind. When my call wasn't answered, I hung up and called right back, but the result was his voicemail.

"This is David... Speak on it..."

"David... Help," I moaned, feeling the tears sliding down my face.

I hung up and dialed 911, but before I could say anything, the sound of a gun going off roared so loud that I jumped and dropped my phone. Out of my peripheral vision, I saw Tesha's body buck from the bullets' impact, and then, a face appeared where her window used to be. I didn't initially recognize the face behind the gun now being aimed at me, but there was something familiar about the madness in the eyes. Florida was the plastic surgery capital of the south, so a person could change anything about their face, but you rarely changed the eyes.

"R-Roland," I whispered, feeling pure terror coursing through me.

"Get out of the car or die right here with your twin."

2 be continued....

I'mma Die Bout Mine 3 (Apex Predators Only)

Lock Down Publications and Ca$h Presents Assisted Publishing Packages

BASIC PACKAGE	UPGRADED PACKAGE
$499	$800
Editing	Typing
Cover Design	Editing
Formatting	Cover Design
	Formatting
ADVANCE PACKAGE	**LDP SUPREME PACKAGE**
$1,200	$1,500
Typing	Typing
Editing	Editing
Cover Design	Cover Design
Formatting	Formatting
Copyright registration	Copyright registration
Proofreading	Proofreading
Upload book to Amazon	Set up Amazon account
	Upload book to Amazon
	Advertise on LDP, Amazon and Facebook Page

***Other services available upon request.
Additional charges may apply
Lock Down Publications
P.O. Box 944
Stockbridge, GA 30281-9998
Phone: 470 303-9761

Submission Guideline

Submit the first three chapters of your completed manuscript to ldpsubmissions@gmail.com, subject line: Your book's title. The manuscript must be in a .doc file and sent as an attachment. Document should be in Times New Roman, double spaced and in size 12 font. Also, provide your synopsis and full contact information. If sending multiple submissions, they must each be in a separate email.

Have a story but no way to send it electronically? You can still submit to LDP/Ca$h Presents. Send in the first three chapters, written or typed, of your completed manuscript to:

LDP: Submissions Dept
Po Box 944
Stockbridge, Ga 30281

DO NOT send original manuscript. Must be a duplicate.

Provide your synopsis and a cover letter containing your full contact information.

Thanks for considering LDP and Ca$h Presents

NEW RELEASES

SOSA GANG 2 by ROMELL TUKES
KINGZ OF THE GAME 7 by PLAYA RAY
SKI MASK MONEY 2 by RENTA
BORN IN THE GRAVE 3 by SELF MADE TAY
LOYALTY IS EVERYTHING 3 by MOLOTTI

Coming Soon from Lock Down Publications/Ca$h Presents

BLOOD OF A BOSS **VI**
SHADOWS OF THE GAME II
TRAP BASTARD II
By Askari
LOYAL TO THE GAME **IV**
By T.J. & Jelissa
TRUE SAVAGE **VIII**
MIDNIGHT CARTEL IV
DOPE BOY MAGIC IV
CITY OF KINGZ III
NIGHTMARE ON SILENT AVE II
THE PLUG OF LIL MEXICO II
CLASSIC CITY II
By Chris Green
BLAST FOR ME **III**
A SAVAGE DOPEBOY III
CUTTHROAT MAFIA III
DUFFLE BAG CARTEL VII
HEARTLESS GOON VI
By Ghost
A HUSTLER'S DECEIT III
KILL ZONE II
BAE BELONGS TO ME III
TIL DEATH II
By Aryanna
KING OF THE TRAP III
By T.J. Edwards
GORILLAZ IN THE BAY V
3X KRAZY III
STRAIGHT BEAST MODE III

De'Kari
KINGPIN KILLAZ IV
STREET KINGS III
PAID IN BLOOD III
CARTEL KILLAZ IV
DOPE GODS III
Hood Rich
SINS OF A HUSTLA II
ASAD
YAYO V
Bred In The Game 2
S. Allen
THE STREETS WILL TALK II
By Yolanda Moore
SON OF A DOPE FIEND III
HEAVEN GOT A GHETTO III
SKI MASK MONEY III
By Renta
LOYALTY AIN'T PROMISED III
By Keith Williams
I'M NOTHING WITHOUT HIS LOVE II
SINS OF A THUG II
TO THE THUG I LOVED BEFORE II
IN A HUSTLER I TRUST II
By Monet Dragun
QUIET MONEY IV
EXTENDED CLIP III
THUG LIFE IV
By Trai'Quan
THE STREETS MADE ME IV
By Larry D. Wright
IF YOU CROSS ME ONCE III
ANGEL V
By Anthony Fields
THE STREETS WILL NEVER CLOSE IV

By K'ajji
HARD AND RUTHLESS III
KILLA KOUNTY IV
By Khufu
MONEY GAME III
By Smoove Dolla
JACK BOYS VS DOPE BOYS IV
A GANGSTA'S QUR'AN V
COKE GIRLZ II
COKE BOYS II
LIFE OF A SAVAGE V
CHI'RAQ GANGSTAS V
SOSA GANG III
BRONX SAVAGES II
BODYMORE KINGPINS II
By Romell Tukes
MURDA WAS THE CASE III
Elijah R. Freeman
AN UNFORESEEN LOVE IV
BABY, I'M WINTERTIME COLD III
By Meesha

QUEEN OF THE ZOO III
By Black Migo
CONFESSIONS OF A JACKBOY III
By Nicholas Lock
KING KILLA II
By Vincent "Vitto" Holloway
BETRAYAL OF A THUG III
By Fre$h
THE MURDER QUEENS III
By Michael Gallon
THE BIRTH OF A GANGSTER III
By Delmont Player
TREAL LOVE II
By Le'Monica Jackson

FOR THE LOVE OF BLOOD III
By Jamel Mitchell
RAN OFF ON DA PLUG II
By Paper Boi Rari
HOOD CONSIGLIERE III
By Keese
PRETTY GIRLS DO NASTY THINGS II
By Nicole Goosby
PROTÉGÉ OF A LEGEND III
LOVE IN THE TRENCHES II
By Corey Robinson
IT'S JUST ME AND YOU II
By Ah'Million
FOREVER GANGSTA III
By Adrian Dulan
GORILLAZ IN THE TRENCHES II
By SayNoMore
THE COCAINE PRINCESS VIII
By King Rio
CRIME BOSS II
Playa Ray
LOYALTY IS EVERYTHING III
Molotti
HERE TODAY GONE TOMORROW II
By Fly Rock
REAL G'S MOVE IN SILENCE II
By Von Diesel
GRIMEY WAYS IV
By Ray Vinci

Available Now

RESTRAINING ORDER **I & II**
By CA$H & Coffee
LOVE KNOWS NO BOUNDARIES **I II & III**
By Coffee
RAISED AS A GOON I, II, III & IV
BRED BY THE SLUMS I, II, III
BLAST FOR ME I & II
ROTTEN TO THE CORE I II III
A BRONX TALE I, II, III
DUFFLE BAG CARTEL I II III IV V VI
HEARTLESS GOON I II III IV V
A SAVAGE DOPEBOY I II
DRUG LORDS I II III
CUTTHROAT MAFIA I II
KING OF THE TRENCHES
By Ghost
LAY IT DOWN **I & II**
LAST OF A DYING BREED I II
BLOOD STAINS OF A SHOTTA I & II III
By Jamaica
LOYAL TO THE GAME I II III
LIFE OF SIN I, II III
By TJ & Jelissa
BLOODY COMMAS I & II
SKI MASK CARTEL I II & III
KING OF NEW YORK I II,III IV V
RISE TO POWER I II III
COKE KINGS I II III IV V
BORN HEARTLESS I II III IV
KING OF THE TRAP I II
By T.J. Edwards
IF LOVING HIM IS WRONG...I & II

LOVE ME EVEN WHEN IT HURTS I II III
By Jelissa
WHEN THE STREETS CLAP BACK I & II III
THE HEART OF A SAVAGE I II III IV
MONEY MAFIA I II
LOYAL TO THE SOIL I II III
By Jibril Williams
A DISTINGUISHED THUG STOLE MY HEART I II
& III
LOVE SHOULDN'T HURT I II III IV
RENEGADE BOYS I II III IV
PAID IN KARMA I II III
SAVAGE STORMS I II III
AN UNFORESEEN LOVE I II III
BABY, I'M WINTERTIME COLD I II
By Meesha
A GANGSTER'S CODE I &, II III
A GANGSTER'S SYN I II III
THE SAVAGE LIFE I II III
CHAINED TO THE STREETS I II III
BLOOD ON THE MONEY I II III
A GANGSTA'S PAIN I II III
By J-Blunt
PUSH IT TO THE LIMIT
By Bre' Hayes
BLOOD OF A BOSS I, II, III, IV, V
SHADOWS OF THE GAME
TRAP BASTARD
By Askari
THE STREETS BLEED MURDER **I, II & III**
THE HEART OF A GANGSTA I II& III
By Jerry Jackson
CUM FOR ME I II III IV V VI VII VIII
An LDP Erotica Collaboration
BRIDE OF A HUSTLA **I II & II**

154

THE FETTI GIRLS **I, II& III**
CORRUPTED BY A GANGSTA I, II III, IV
BLINDED BY HIS LOVE
THE PRICE YOU PAY FOR LOVE I, II ,III
DOPE GIRL MAGIC I II III
By Destiny Skai
WHEN A GOOD GIRL GOES BAD
By Adrienne
THE COST OF LOYALTY I II III
By Kweli
A GANGSTER'S REVENGE **I II III & IV**
THE BOSS MAN'S DAUGHTERS I II III IV V
A SAVAGE LOVE **I & II**
BAE BELONGS TO ME I II
A HUSTLER'S DECEIT I, II, III
WHAT BAD BITCHES DO I, II, III
SOUL OF A MONSTER I II III
KILL ZONE
A DOPE BOY'S QUEEN I II III
TIL DEATH
By Aryanna
A KINGPIN'S AMBITON
A KINGPIN'S AMBITION **II**
I MURDER FOR THE DOUGH
By Ambitious
TRUE SAVAGE I II III IV V VI VII
DOPE BOY MAGIC I, II, III
MIDNIGHT CARTEL I II III
CITY OF KINGZ I II
NIGHTMARE ON SILENT AVE
THE PLUG OF LIL MEXICO II
CLASSIC CITY
By Chris Green
A DOPEBOY'S PRAYER
By Eddie "Wolf" Lee

THE KING CARTEL **I, II & III**
By Frank Gresham
THESE NIGGAS AIN'T LOYAL **I, II & III**
By Nikki Tee
GANGSTA SHYT **I II &III**
By CATO
THE ULTIMATE BETRAYAL
By Phoenix
Boss'n Up i , ii & IIi
By Royal Nicole
I LOVE YOU TO DEATH
By Destiny J
I RIDE FOR MY HITTA
I STILL RIDE FOR MY HITTA
By Misty Holt
LOVE & CHASIN' PAPER
By Qay Crockett
TO DIE IN VAIN
SINS OF A HUSTLA
By ASAD
BROOKLYN HUSTLAZ
By Boogsy Morina
BROOKLYN ON LOCK I & II
By Sonovia
GANGSTA CITY
By Teddy Duke
A DRUG KING AND HIS DIAMOND I & II III
A DOPEMAN'S RICHES
HER MAN, MINE'S TOO I, II
CASH MONEY HO'S
THE WIFEY I USED TO BE I II
PRETTY GIRLS DO NASTY THINGS
By Nicole Goosby
TRAPHOUSE KING **I II & III**
KINGPIN KILLAZ I II III

STREET KINGS I II
PAID IN BLOOD **I II**
CARTEL KILLAZ I II III
DOPE GODS I II
By Hood Rich
LIPSTICK KILLAH **I, II, III**
CRIME OF PASSION I II & III
FRIEND OR FOE I II III
By Mimi
STEADY MOBBN' **I, II, III**
THE STREETS STAINED MY SOUL I II III
By Marcellus Allen
WHO SHOT YA **I, II, III**
SON OF A DOPE FIEND I II
HEAVEN GOT A GHETTO I II
SKI MASK MONEY I II
Renta
GORILLAZ IN THE BAY **I II III IV**
TEARS OF A GANGSTA I II
3X KRAZY I II
STRAIGHT BEAST MODE I II
DE'KARI
TRIGGADALE I II III
MURDAROBER WAS THE CASE I II
Elijah R. Freeman
GOD BLESS THE TRAPPERS I, II, III
THESE SCANDALOUS STREETS I, II, III
FEAR MY GANGSTA I, II, III IV, V
THESE STREETS DON'T LOVE NOBODY I, II
BURY ME A G I, II, III, IV, V
A GANGSTA'S EMPIRE I, II, III, IV
THE DOPEMAN'S BODYGAURD I II
THE REALEST KILLAZ I II III
THE LAST OF THE OGS I II III
Tranay Adams
THE STREETS ARE CALLING

Duquie Wilson
MARRIED TO A BOSS I II III
By Destiny Skai & Chris Green
KINGZ OF THE GAME I II III IV V VI VII
CRIME BOSS
Playa Ray
SLAUGHTER GANG I II III
RUTHLESS HEART I II III
By Willie Slaughter
FUK SHYT
By Blakk Diamond
DON'T F#CK WITH MY HEART I II
By Linnea
ADDICTED TO THE DRAMA I II III
IN THE ARM OF HIS BOSS II
By Jamila
YAYO I II III IV
A SHOOTER'S AMBITION I II
BRED IN THE GAME
By S. Allen
TRAP GOD I II III
RICH $AVAGE I II III
MONEY IN THE GRAVE I II III
By Martell Troublesome Bolden
FOREVER GANGSTA I II
 GLOCKS ON SATIN SHEETS I II
By Adrian Dulan
TOE TAGZ I II III IV
LEVELS TO THIS SHYT I II
IT'S JUST ME AND YOU
By Ah'Million
KINGPIN DREAMS I II III
RAN OFF ON DA PLUG
By Paper Boi Rari
CONFESSIONS OF A GANGSTA I II III IV

CONFESSIONS OF A JACKBOY I II
By Nicholas Lock
I'M NOTHING WITHOUT HIS LOVE
SINS OF A THUG
TO THE THUG I LOVED BEFORE
A GANGSTA SAVED XMAS
IN A HUSTLER I TRUST
By Monet Dragun
CAUGHT UP IN THE LIFE I II III
THE STREETS NEVER LET GO I II III
By Robert Baptiste
NEW TO THE GAME I II III
MONEY, MURDER & MEMORIES I II III
By Malik D. Rice
LIFE OF A SAVAGE I II III IV
A GANGSTA'S QUR'AN I II III IV
MURDA SEASON I II III
GANGLAND CARTEL I II III
CHI'RAQ GANGSTAS I II III IV
KILLERS ON ELM STREET I II III
JACK BOYZ N DA BRONX I II III
A DOPEBOY'S DREAM I II III
JACK BOYS VS DOPE BOYS I II III
COKE GIRLZ
COKE BOYS
SOSA GANG I II
BRONX SAVAGES
BODYMORE KINGPINS
By Romell Tukes
LOYALTY AIN'T PROMISED I II
By Keith Williams
QUIET MONEY I II III
THUG LIFE I II III
EXTENDED CLIP I II
A GANGSTA'S PARADISE

By Trai'Quan
THE STREETS MADE ME I II III
By Larry D. Wright
THE ULTIMATE SACRIFICE I, II, III, IV, V, VI
KHADIFI
IF YOU CROSS ME ONCE I II
ANGEL I II III IV
IN THE BLINK OF AN EYE
By Anthony Fields
THE LIFE OF A HOOD STAR
By Ca$h & Rashia Wilson
THE STREETS WILL NEVER CLOSE I II III
By K'ajji
CREAM I II III
THE STREETS WILL TALK
By Yolanda Moore
NIGHTMARES OF A HUSTLA I II III
By King Dream
CONCRETE KILLA I II III
VICIOUS LOYALTY I II III
By Kingpen
HARD AND RUTHLESS I II
MOB TOWN 251
THE BILLIONAIRE BENTLEYS I II III
REAL G'S MOVE IN SILENCE
By Von Diesel
GHOST MOB
Stilloan Robinson
MOB TIES I II III IV V VI
SOUL OF A HUSTLER, HEART OF A KILLER I II
GORILLAZ IN THE TRENCHES
By SayNoMore
BODYMORE MURDERLAND I II III
THE BIRTH OF A GANGSTER I II
By Delmont Player

FOR THE LOVE OF A BOSS
By C. D. Blue
MOBBED UP I II III IV
THE BRICK MAN I II III IV V
THE COCAINE PRINCESS I II III IV V VI VII
By King Rio
KILLA KOUNTY I II III IV
By Khufu
MONEY GAME I II
By Smoove Dolla
A GANGSTA'S KARMA I II III
By FLAME
KING OF THE TRENCHES I II III
 by GHOST & TRANAY ADAMS
QUEEN OF THE ZOO I II
By Black Migo
GRIMEY WAYS I II III
By Ray Vinci
XMAS WITH AN ATL SHOOTER
By Ca$h & Destiny Skai
KING KILLA
By Vincent "Vitto" Holloway
BETRAYAL OF A THUG I II
By Fre$h
THE MURDER QUEENS I II
By Michael Gallon
TREAL LOVE
By Le'Monica Jackson
FOR THE LOVE OF BLOOD I II
By Jamel Mitchell
HOOD CONSIGLIERE I II
By Keese
PROTÉGÉ OF A LEGEND I II
LOVE IN THE TRENCHES
By Corey Robinson
BORN IN THE GRAVE I II III

By Self Made Tay
MOAN IN MY MOUTH
By XTASY
TORN BETWEEN A GANGSTER AND A
GENTLEMAN
By J-BLUNT & Miss Kim
LOYALTY IS EVERYTHING I II
Molotti
HERE TODAY GONE TOMORROW
By Fly Rock
PILLOW PRINCESS
By S. Hawkins

BOOKS BY LDP'S CEO, CA$H

TRUST IN NO MAN
TRUST IN NO MAN 2
TRUST IN NO MAN 3
BONDED BY BLOOD
SHORTY GOT A THUG
THUGS CRY
THUGS CRY 2
THUGS CRY 3
TRUST NO BITCH
TRUST NO BITCH 2
TRUST NO BITCH 3
TIL MY CASKET DROPS
RESTRAINING ORDER
RESTRAINING ORDER 2
IN LOVE WITH A CONVICT
LIFE OF A HOOD STAR
XMAS WITH AN ATL SHOOTER